I couldn't understand what was wrong. . . .

Leslie hadn't taken her arms from around her mother's neck, and now Mary buried her face in her daughter's hair. I remembered reading in her journal about how she longed to hold her children. Why wasn't she smiling? Why wasn't she thanking me? Without lifting her face to me, her eyes rolled in her head and she stared at me. I can still remember the weakness that grew greater and greater in my knees and calf muscles. Slowly her head rose up, the stare never leaving the bones of my face. I would turn to ashes from her look and flake to the floor. She wet her dry lips and spoke to me.

She said, "You have ruined everything, you miserable child."

Other Bantam Starfire Books you will enjoy

HOLDING
ME HERE

PAM CONRAD

BANTAM BOOKS
TORONTO • NEW YORK • LONDON • SYDNEY • AUCKLAND

RL 5, IL age 12 and up

This low-priced Bantam Book
has been completely reset in a type face
designed for easy reading, and was printed
from new plates. It contains the complete
text of the original hard-cover edition.
NOT ONE WORD HAS BEEN OMITTED.

HOLDING ME HERE
A Bantam Book / published by arrangement with
Harper & Row, Publishers Inc.

PRINTING HISTORY
Harper & Row edition published April 1986

Bantam edition / June 1987

ISBN 0-553-26525-3

Published simultaneously in the United States and Canada

Bantam Books are published by Bantam Books, Inc. Its trademark, consisting
of the words "Bantam Books" and the portrayal of a rooster, is Registered
in U.S. Patent and Trademark Office and in other countries. Marca Regis-
trada. Bantam Books, Inc., 666 Fifth Avenue, New York, New York 10103.

PRINTED IN THE UNITED STATES OF AMERICA

O   0 1 2 3 4 5 6 7 8 9

for you, DeeDee, wherever you are

1

I'm not sure where to begin. I guess I should start at the beginning of November that year, the day the boarder moved in, although that might not be it at all. Maybe the real beginning was when my parents decided to get a divorce, and my father moved out. Who knows? Who ever said life was simple? Not me. Not anymore, that's for sure.

Anyway, I was in the kitchen the afternoon the boarder was expected. Ma and I had come to a sort of uneasy truce about the whole thing. I was dead set against renting out my old playroom, but Ma said that unless I was prepared to go out and get a job, any decision involving money was up to her. I was only fourteen, and Ma knew I was not exactly in a position to rake in the dough. So there I was, hanging out, and waiting for this boarder to arrive. I was doing a health project at the table about intestines, and my mother was making some of her crazy salt dough baskets that she had decided to give absolutely everyone for Christmas.

"What's she like?" I asked. "Tell me again."

"I told you already. She seems very private. She's quiet, pleasant, and she's a nurse at Mercy Hospital. She says she has all kinds of odd hours because she's new, and she'll get the rough shifts for a while."

"But is she glamorous? Does she look rich? Mysterious?"

Ma didn't skip a beat in her kneading. The big

wad of dough rolled and folded and stretched under her hands. It was really beautiful, all white and puffy looking. "Rich?" Ma laughed and rubbed her nose with the back of her hand. "Why would she be renting a room in a house in Rockland Acres if she was rich, Robin?"

"You never know, Ma. Maybe she's some—what's the word? Eclectic? Exotic?"

"You mean eccentric?"

"Yeah, some eccentric rich woman, who is hiding from her father's team of lawyers who are trying to force her to run the family corporation."

"What an imagination you have."

"Or maybe she's a famous journalist from a big national magazine or a TV show, and she's come to spy on the typical American family. She'll hide in the hamper in the bathroom, in the garage, under the dining room table at holiday dinners, taking notes. This nurse thing is probably just a front. I'll bet she could afford to stay in the Garden Village Hotel if she wanted to. She doesn't need my old playroom to slum around in."

Ma just shook her head and went on kneading. "Oh, Robin," she said. She used to say that all the time, "Oh, Robin," like I had a lot to learn, and I was getting on her nerves.

"And besides, what if I want to set up my tent indoors? You know that's the only room I can do it in."

"Really, Robin. When was the last time you set up the tent indoors? Three, four years ago?"

I decided to drop it. I twisted my red rubber tubing into small intestine shapes on the table, and Ma kept pounding her dough.

When we heard the unfamiliar sound of a car pulling past the kitchen window and driving into the back, I peered out and tried to see, but it was getting dark outside, five o'clock and dark already. I hate the winter, always have. It's not the cold, it's the dark.

The headlights went out, and I sat back at the table, trying to look casual amidst the red tubing, the clouds of flour, and lumps of dough. It suddenly occurred to me that this lady might take one look at our kitchen and change her mind about staying. I was hopeful that the giant display box of Camel cigarettes on top of the refrigerator and the picture of Sylvester Stallone Ma had taped to the refrigerator door might give the boarder second thoughts.

We listened to the screen door open and waited for the bell. Then I ran to let her in. I don't know what I had expected, but it wasn't what I saw. She couldn't have been an heiress or a journalist in a million years. She looked more like Gretel, lost in the woods.

"Hi," I said. "I'm Robin Lewis. Come on in."

She put down her two suitcases right there in the doorway and extended her hand to me. She smiled, and I saw that under her lost look she was really kind of pretty. She was younger than my mother, skinnier, and she seemed almost bloodless, she was so pale. "It's nice to meet you, Robin. My name is Mary Walker. Is it okay if I leave my car back by the garage? Is that the best place?"

"Sure," I said, as I picked up one of her suitcases. "Anywhere is fine, just as long as it's off the street by midnight. They give tickets around here." I led her into the kitchen, which despite the weird chaos, felt warm and welcoming.

Ma had washed her hands. She was drying them and smiling. "Hi, Mary. I'm glad you made it before the rain started tonight." They smiled at each other and nodded, a peculiar way I noticed women have sometimes of not shaking hands. It's like there's some kind of unspoken code about who you shake hands with, who you kiss, who you hug, and the rest you kind of nod at. Ma offered her a cup of coffee, and they talked small talk about the weather, the roads in town, and the best place to buy anti-freeze before it was too late. I cleaned up my health project and listened. No, she wasn't an heiress or a journalist, that was certain. I was beginning to think that maybe she was someone who had been wandering around with amnesia, and she didn't know who she really was, or maybe she had just been released from prison, after spending ten years there for something she didn't do. I was surprised to find myself feeling sorry for her.

Even so, it was uncomfortable to have a stranger in the house. I knew I wasn't going to like it. Not that I didn't have enough privacy in our big old house, but, I don't know, it could get kind of de-pressing, having someone you don't even know actually living in your house. And something about Mary Walker was so sad and lost-looking that I was afraid it was going to rub off somehow on the doorknobs, or seep into my room. But there was an opposite little tugging inside me too, that made me want to help her somehow, to bring a little sunshine into her life. A real Pollyanna, right?

After a while, Ma suggested I help Mary carry her suitcases up to the room, and at the very instant I stood, the phone rang right next to me on the kitchen wall, and I answered it.

"Hi, Janet," said a man's deep voice. "How's it going?"

"This isn't Janet," I answered. "This is Robin." I waited.

"Oh. Sorry. Is Janet there?"

"Yes, my *mother*'s right here," I answered. "Who should I say is calling?"

"Tom."

I held the phone out to my mother, and its long cord bounced silently on the floor. "It's Tom, for you," I whispered. "Who is Tom?"

She didn't even answer me. She kind of closed her eyes as if to dismiss me and took the phone. "Please help Mary with her suitcases, Robin. Thank you." Just like that. A strange man calls the house, with a voice like a cowboy in a bad movie, and I get a please, a thank you, and that's all, folks.

I helped Mary with one of the suitcases, and then with a couple of boxes of books and things from the car, hardly saying a word. Usually I'm pretty talkative, but every time we went through the kitchen I was trying to hear what my mother was laughing and talking about, and when we weren't in the kitchen my wheels were going a mile a minute.

I guess in those days I felt that my life was slipping away from me, changing in ways I couldn't control. Helping lost-in-the-woods Gretel up the stairs, I got to thinking about witches and fairies and wishes, and I remember that if I could have made a wish then, and had it come true, I would have wished it were summer, three years before, and I would have wished my father were in the backyard, starting the fire for a barbecue, and wished my mother were making macaroni salad with shrimp, and there would be no boarder in our house, and no man named Tom on the phone.

2

Ma had made it very clear that I was to stay out of the new boarder's room. She even ran a lecture past me about privacy, and how I wouldn't want my privacy invaded, so I should respect someone else's. I thought about all this as I stood outside Mary's room, and how it used to be my old playroom where I had kept my dollhouse and my doll collection, but now it was empty of any signs of me, and we called it Mary's room. So much for *my* privacy.

I'd always liked my playroom. It had three big windows with soft lace curtains, and pale-blue shades that pulled down at night. I knew the room would be bright now, with the early winter snow falling silently outside, leaving soppy white cushions like Ma's dough on the windowsills.

I stood silently before the closed door and listened to myself breathing. No one was in the house. Mary had left an hour before, Ma was at work and not expected home until much later, and everything was very quiet except for the occasional hiss of a hot radiator. I stood there trying to decide. If I could reach back into the past to tell the old Robin something, I would have grabbed her by the throat right then and said, "Butt out, kiddo. Before it's too late. This is none of your business." It was bad enough snooping through Ma's address book for the infamous Tom, but snooping in a stranger's room was just low. I know that now.

Like a magician's assistant in a trance, my hand reached out of its own accord, and my fingers wrapped around the doorknob. I just stood there like that, waiting to see what I would do next. I turned the knob.

I stepped into the room and closed the door behind me without a sound. It smelled different. Mary Walker had only lived with us for two days and already there was an unfamiliar soapy smell in the air, as if she had been blowing bubbles at night. There was nothing lying around out in the open, so I went right to the dresser and silently pulled out the top drawer.

I wasn't too surprised by anything I saw. Mary was always in her nurse's uniform, and in the drawer were the usual white nurse's stockings, plain underwear, and what looked like some old jewelry, the kind you might get from a great-grandmother or something. I wrapped a long gold and pearl necklace around my neck and looked at myself in the mirror above the dresser. I opened my eyes wide and innocent and puckered my mouth slightly. "Why, Doctor Kidney, I'd be delighted to meet you after the operation for dinner. At six you say? Certainly. I'll be ready."

I carefully lifted one of the bras and passed my arms through the straps. This Mary was skinny, but she was bigger than Ma in the chest category. Even with my sweat shirt on over my own chest, I didn't come close to filling her bra.

I dropped the necklace and the bra back in the drawer and went on to open one of the bottom drawers. There were two pale-colored sweaters, as soft and as warm as baby rabbits. I lifted one to my face. It tickled my nose, and for a minute I thought I would sneeze, until I saw the pictures that were under it. They were in a double frame that was hinged in the middle—two photos of two little kids, the kind of pictures they take in school, showing clean faces, slicked back hair, and unreal smiles.

One picture was of a little girl, about ten years old. She had whitish-blond hair and little barrettes holding her hair away from her face. She was wearing a funny stiff-looking dress that had her name, Leslie, embroidered on the trim. And she was smiling. That is, her mouth was smiling, like someone had just told her, "Smile," but her eyes looked sad, and even at that point I saw that old lost-in-the-woods look again. Leslie.

The other picture was of a little boy, about seven. He was the type that I would have tied up in his room, with the excuse that we were playing Indians, if I had to babysit him. Trouble, I could tell. And there was something about the shape of the cheek and chin that said these two kids were related, probably sister and brother, and probably in the same school because the backdrop was the same.

At that instant I heard Ma's old muffler-free bomb pull in the driveway, and I panicked. She was early and my instinct was to bolt out of the room, but I controlled myself, and carefully put the pictures back, the sweater, slid the drawers quietly shut, and left the room, closing the door behind me. My heart was pounding in my throat, and I went to my room to compose myself a minute before I went down to say hello.

I didn't have to wait long. Ma came looking for me. "Robin?"

"Come on in, Ma," I said, plopping on the bed and spreading my books around to look as if I had been there for hours. She opened the door and looked in at me. She was still wearing her coat and her hat, and her cheeks were all rosy and cold looking. Every once in a while I see my mother fresh, as if I didn't know her, and I know I'd like her. "You're early," I said, instead of—"I like you."

"Something wrong?"

"Yes." She sat on the bed and unzipped her jacket. Then she turned and looked at me with a faintly glassy stare. "I couldn't concentrate at work. Something's been bothering me, and I need to talk to you about it. We have to talk about privacy and secrets."

Privacy and secrets. What did she have, ESP or something? Had she been sitting at her desk at work and known suddenly that I was snooping around Mary's room? I sat stone still and felt my cheeks and armpits prickle with fear. "What about it?"

She took a deep breath, and said, as if she had been rehearsing it all day, "I would like to have privacy, but not secrets."

I waited.

She waited.

"What are you talking about?" I finally asked.

"I felt bad the other day when you asked me who Tom was, and I didn't answer you. I just wasn't sure how to talk about it. I didn't answer you, and I didn't feel good about it."

I was beginning to wish she had said, "I looked in my magic mirror and saw you snooping in Mary's room."

"I guess I need to talk to you about something," she continued. "You see, when Daddy and I got divorced, I read a lot of books about the best things to do for kids when a marriage is breaking up."

I began piling up my books neatly, not looking at her.

"One of the things I read was that when a divorced parent brings dates into the home, the children tend to look at each date as a potential replacement parent, and this can be really confusing."

"So? *You* don't date," I said with some assurance.

"I do. Sometimes." She slipped off her coat and lay across my bed with her chin propped in her hands. I didn't like how she was getting so chummy and acting like a teenager. What was she going to tell me next, that she and Tom were going steady? Was she going to start writing "Tom and Janet" on the bathroom mirror with lipstick?

"You never told me that." I could hear the whine, and I coughed lightly, hoping to cover it.

"Well, that's what I'm talking about. Privacy and secrets. I guess I've been keeping my dating secret this past year or so, and now I don't want it to be a secret, but I would still like it to be private."

"Are you going to marry Tom?" It was one of those questions I didn't want answered, but it fell out of my mouth before I could stop it.

"You see?" she said, sitting up and pointing a finger at me. "You immediately assume that because I date someone I'm going to marry him and you're going to have to live with him."

"Well, aren't you? Won't I?"

"No. I'm not. And Tom's not the only one I have dated, or intend to date."

"That's disgusting."

Ma looked at me hard. "I'm sorry you feel that way, Robin. I had hoped you'd understand. I thought maybe you were ready, so that I wouldn't have to be secretive anymore. I was hoping I could just have privacy without feeling that I'm sneaking around behind your back, because I love you, and I always try to be honest with you."

We looked at each other, and it was a good thing her cheeks were so red, because it made her look human, and made me want to hug her. I guess we both thought the same thing, because next thing I knew we had our arms around each other's neck, and her cold cheek was pressed against my neck. "I'm just trying to do the right thing, Robin. It's so hard."

"I know. I know," I said. "I'm sorry. Just promise me one thing, Ma. No, two things."

"Sure. What?"

"Don't date any of my teachers, and if you ever go out with Sylvester Stallone, I want to go, too."

Ma exploded into hysterical laughter and pushed me back on the bed where she tried to smother me with my pillow. "Okay," she laughed, breathless, "it's a deal. I feel better now. Come on." She stood up next to the bed. "What do you say we go get a pizza and have an early dinner? I'm starved."

I'm telling you, she could have passed for a fourteen-year-old anywhere, and I wasn't so sure I liked it.

3

When my father first moved out, two and a half years before Mary came to live with us, I used to go stay at his apartment in the city every weekend. I can remember how exciting it was in the beginning. My parents would say things to me like, "Just think, it's like you have two homes, two special places to be, where you belong. You're so lucky."

Well, it didn't work out exactly like that. My father's place wasn't really mine at all. I was a visitor, and when I went there, he would pull out the rollaway bed. Now, I don't call that a second home. A real home is where you get to pick the wallpaper for your room, and where you get your mail. But it's okay, I guess. Not great, but okay.

It's been hard with my father. I can't really explain it. When we all lived together, I felt fine around him. But now that he's gone, when we're together I feel we don't have too much in common. It's as if you have this favorite old stuffed chair that you love and always watch TV in, and one day the chair gets moved to another room, and you never sit in it anymore. It's not that you don't love the chair anymore. It's just that it's not where you need it most.

He's kind of an interesting guy though, I guess. A little dull, but interesting, like a fossil of a moth

in an old rock. He's a professor of paleontology at
the university in the city, and that's where he lives
now, right near the campus. Once in a while he
goes on an expedition somewhere, but he just digs
in one little spot for weeks with a small shovel and
little brushes.

I really don't know what my mother and father
ever saw in each other. They're direct opposites,
which I thought was supposed to attract, and maybe
it does, but I guess it can wear off. For instance,
even living alone, every breakfast, lunch, and dinner, my father will set the table, sit down and eat,
and then get up and clear things off and wash everything. My mother is the reverse. Either she grabs
a bite when the mood hits her, or she'll plop down
with a tray of cold cuts for us in front of the TV,
or she'll just snack all day on fruit and cheese and
popcorn. And my mother washes the dishes when
she runs out of clean ones. I guess that's why they
drove each other nuts.

Where do I fit in? I don't know. It feels safe to
have everything so predictable like my father, but
I guess I'm more like my mother when it comes
to lifestyles. When you live with someone it's hard
to tell if you do things because that's the way you
want them yourself or if you're just accustomed to
the way the other person does things.

Anyway, I used to go to his place every weekend, but there really wasn't much to do, and I got
busy with my friends on some weekends. So as
time passed, it evolved to every other weekend,
and sometimes I didn't sleep over at all, but just
visited for the day, and then came home to my
own bed. I had never wondered about it before,
but after the talk with my mother about all her

dates, I started to wonder if she was dating while I was safely at my father's overnight. I didn't want to think about it.

The weekend after my excursion into Mary's room and my talk with Ma about her social life, I was supposed to spend the weekend at my father's. He, by the way, had no need for privacy. His life was an open book to me; I could go through any of his drawers or closets, and ask anything I wanted. He had nothing to hide. After a few weekends of exploring every corner of his new apartment life, I was totally bored.

I got to his apartment that morning, taking the train and a cab all by myself. He had given me a key, and I let myself in. There was a note on the hall table. "Robin. I have run over to my office for some work. I'll be back shortly. 9:00 A.M. Dad."

It was ten o'clock and the university was within walking distance, so I set to work quickly. I had been wanting some time alone in his place, and I knew exactly what to do. I moved his small fossil display case away from the front of the big living-room window, and I put the lamp closer to his overstuffed chair. Once the area was clear, I dragged over the small oriental rug from the hall and placed it in the middle. Then I carried the two chairs and the kitchen table from the "eating area," as he called it, and placed them right in front of the bright window. Sunshine poured onto the reddish wood, and it glowed. There. It looked much better. He really had no sense of how to make a place feel homey.

I had just taken a vase of old dried flowers off the top of his bookcase and put it in the center of the table when he came through the door. He was carrying a stack of books and looked over the top of them at me with his pipe in his mouth. "Robin! You're here!" We smiled at each other, and I crossed the room to kiss him hello. He slid some of the books off his stack into my arms. "Here. Help me with these. I need to go over some things before Monday."

He stopped suddenly and looked at my new furniture arrangement. He said, "Hmph," and I looked at the room with him. "I like it," he added. "Yes, that's just what this room needed, a nice sitting spot right in the sunshine. Very nice, Robin. Good thinking."

Even though he's pretty boring, him saying something like that can last me for days. A compliment from him is something I can carry around and pull out when I need it. "Come on," I said, "put your books on the table, and you can work there in the sun."

"No," he said, putting the pipe in his hand, "I eat at the table. I work at my desk."

"Oh, Dad. I'll bet your socks even match."

"What kind of thing is that to say?" He was smiling and looking at me as if he were trying to figure me out, as if to say, "Now what is this peculiar rock formation we have here?"

"Have you had breakfast yet?" he asked. "How about some nice fresh bagels and jelly?"

I laughed. That was one of the few things Ma was strict about. You don't put jelly on bagels. Just cream cheese or butter. She once told me it was because he was from the Midwest that he did something so gross. "Sure," I said. "I haven't had bagels and jelly in weeks."

"Pineapple okay?" he asked.

"Super."

I sat at the table while he puttered around the

kitchen. He pulled the toaster down from the cabinet. He wouldn't dream of just leaving it sitting
there on the counter all day. I liked watching him.
"Dad."

"Yes, Bird."

"Did you know Ma dates?" Talk about impulsive.

He plugged in the toaster as if he hadn't heard
me and carefully split a bagel with a knife.

"Huh? Did you?"

"Well, not for certain. But I assumed she would.
Your mother's an attractive woman. Lively. I guess
she would date."

"What's that got to do with it? Attractive. Lively.
I know plenty of attractive, lively mothers who
find better ways to spend their time than to date.
I couldn't believe it when I found out."

"How did you find out?"

"She told me. You know Ma. Always getting
into feelings and truth."

He kind of snorted.

"Well?"

"Well, what?"

"Do *you* date?"

He placed the jelly on the table in front of me
and positioned two small china plates with knives
and napkins and juice glasses. "What exactly do
you mean by date?"

I couldn't believe him. "You know—date! It's
where you take a strange lady out and do things
with her!"

He put his hands in his pockets, and the corner
of his mouth twitched. "On my honor, Bird, I
have never taken out a strange lady and done things
with her."

"Dad. You know what I mean. Do you see ladies? Do you have women friends? Are you going to get someone to replace Ma?" I was sorry I had brought it all up. I didn't realize how it was going to upset me, and I could hear my voice crack. My eyes clouded up.

The bagel popped up in the toaster. Lucky Dad. It gave him an excuse to turn his back to me and think. He was quiet, until he came to the table with two bagels speared on a knife. He put one on each of our plates and sat down across from me. "The truth," he said, as if it were a chapter title. "I have been invited to a few dinners where there have been available ladies present, but—"

"You don't date."

"No. I guess not."

Now you talk about your crazies in the world. Would you believe me if I told you that hearing that made me feel sad? There's no pleasing me, right? I got this awful feeling that my father had been left behind somehow. That his life was empty and dull, and I guess it showed on my face because he patted my hand and smiled at me reassuringly.

"But I'm happy, Bird. I really am. This is what's comfortable for me right now. I have my teaching, and my projects, and did I tell you this summer I'll be going to Arizona on a special expedition to Monument Valley with the graduate class? We're going to construct a paleographic map of the area."

He went on and on, and he didn't look lonely at all. As a matter of fact, he looked happy and kind of contented in a warm, woollen sort of way. Me, I ate my bagel and tried to keep the jelly from leaking out the hole. Ma says that's why you're not supposed to put jelly on bagels. They weren't made for that.

4

As usual, that year the ninth grade had a big project to sell holiday cards and wrapping paper. Our student council is chock-full of wonderful ideas like that, as if I didn't have enough to do with homework and helping out at home. Now I had to go door-to-door as well, pushing Santa paper and red and green pom-poms on all my neighbors. It wasn't great quality stuff, and when people placed an order with me, I was sure it was out of politeness.

I had just gotten home from school with my pile of books and about a hundred slick catalogues showing all my goodies. Ma had left a note on the table. "Stir the sauce. Gone to cleaners. M." The house smelled wonderful. I stirred the sauce and tasted it, and then ran upstairs for my slippers. Mary had left her door open a crack, and I stopped in the hall and stared at it. I just stood there. Ma was due home any minute. Mary was at work, the three to midnight shift, and I knew there were a few other drawers I wanted to check out. And the desk. I hadn't looked in the desk yet. I walked to the door and pressed my hand to the wooden molding and ran my finger over the ornate doorknob. "Leslie," I said out loud. Who was Leslie?

Maybe Mary's family had all died in a terrible house fire. One day she had just run to the candy store to get a magazine, and the kids were sleeping soundly. But while she was gone, the old oil furnace backfired, smoked, and in seconds the house was in flames. She saw the smoke and the brilliant light from the corner, and the neighbors had had to restrain her from running into the inferno. Later the firemen had carried out Leslie and her brother, two charred bodies, wrapped in orange bags. Ever since then, Mary had wandered around from room to rented room, guilt-ridden and despondent.

Or maybe Mary's children had been kidnapped, and she got the job in a hospital hoping that someday, a child would be brought into the emergency ward with a broken arm or a deep cut, and it would be Leslie, and they would recognize each other and fly into each other's arms. "Mommy!" "Leslie!" My eyes filled with tears, and I pulled the door shut from the outside. Maybe later. Maybe if Ma went out.

I heard Ma come in downstairs, and I heard her dial the phone. I don't know why, but I hesitated on the steps and listened. She spoke in a low voice. I couldn't make out the words, and then I realized she had taken the long cord into the laundry room and closed the door. I had always thought before that she did it because I was too noisy, and she couldn't hear. Now I knew what it really was. Privacy. What did my mother do on a date? And when would *I* date? Wouldn't it be gross to double date? We could go to a movie or a rock concert and then out for a hamburger and a Coke. I shivered. I had seen my mother dance, bopping around the house to some of her old records. I hoped she didn't go out dancing where anyone I knew would see her.

She was hanging up the phone by the time I got to the kitchen. I stirred the sauce, and watched her out of the corner of my eye. "Who was that?"

"Who was what?"

"On the phone."

She turned off the water in the sink and looked at me. "Is this what we do, check on each other? Inform each other about every phone call? Both of us?"

"Yes," I said, but I knew she never grilled me about my friends or phone calls. "I think that's fair. Besides, I feel safer somehow knowing who you're talking to."

She said, "Tom," simply, and went on with her dishwashing. "We've run out of glasses. Do you have any in your room?" She knew I didn't. The sink was full of glasses. "I see you've got this year's holiday wrap catalogues. Have you sold anything yet?"

"No. I just got them today and I came right home."

"Maybe Mary would like to see what you have," she offered. "You should stick one under her door."

"Mary?" I asked, as if that was the last person I'd think of. "Why would she need wrap or cards? Maybe she doesn't even have any family or friends. Why would she be living here if she had friends?"

"Oh, Robin," she said. "People who rent rooms are not the lost roaming misfits of the world. Some are just in transition, or in a period of their lives where 'home' is not a priority. But I'm sure she has friends."

"Has she told you? Does she talk to you at all about her life, or where she came from? Her family?"

"She said she's from Denver. She has family there, a couple of sisters, I think, and she said she plans to stay here a year or two so she can save up some money and maybe buy a small house over near the hospital."

"A house? Just for herself?"

"Robin. That's enough. What difference does it make to you? It's none of your business."

"Well, I don't want to ask her about the wrappings. I don't think she has any friends, and I think I would embarrass her. She probably doesn't even know anybody to send a card to."

"Then she must have landed here on a flying saucer two weeks ago."

I stared at Ma. "I never thought of that."

Ma threw a towel right at me. "Set the table, would you? And get all these catalogues away. I'm going to ask you to clean up tonight, too. I promised Jackie I'd go see a movie with her later."

So, Ma would be going out that night with her friend from work. Already my wheels were spinning. I was thinking about Leslie. I moved the catalogues to my chair, but it had little effect on the amount of room on the table. I set two TV trays for us, and put them on the kitchen sink. Who's fussy?

I put the double bolt on the door when Ma left. That way if she or Mary came back early they'd have to ring the bell for me to open the door. I turned on a lot of lights and the TV. I put a glass of soda in front of the tube and double-stepped up the stairs to Mary's room. The door opened easily, and this time I left it open so I wouldn't have to turn on a light. I just hoped no one from the outside would see the room glowing faintly from the hall light.

There was a jacket lying on the bed and two

shopping bags, partially unpacked. I wasn't much interested in new stuff. I wanted to know about her past, and I went straight for the desk. It rolled open noisily, and I cringed. Inside there were a few pads, a small stack of travelers' checks, and some makeup. I pushed around, digging my fingers into dark corners, back recesses, and I touched something leather, thick. My heart began to pound. It was a diary, and I drew it slowly out and held it in my hand. There was a small clasp on it, but it wasn't locked. I carried it to the doorway and sat down under the hall light. This was it. I kept my ears wide open for any sounds, and I opened to the first page.

Mary's handwriting was very small and tight, but there was a haunting perfection about it, as if it had been stamped out by a machine. Every a, every b, was exactly like the others. I began reading.

JANUARY 1

Ted took the kids to his mother's for lunch and it gave me time to clean up around here. The chaos starts to get to me after a while. But it was good to have a few days off from work to catch up. The Christmas tree looks so lovely again this year. I keep asking myself why I don't feel happy. Leslie wanted to sleep with us again last night and Ted was hard on her. She hears so much of what goes on. I am frightened for her. Once he was asleep, I went and lay down by her in her own bed. She was shivering. She tells me she's cold. I wonder if it's normal for her to tremble so often. Timmy seems oblivious. He's my happy-go-lucky kid, except I think he broke Leslie's radio on purpose. But how can I tell? Maybe he didn't. My New Year's resolution is to look

for the good. I'm so negative. I read in the paper today:
Two men looked out from prison bars, one saw mud,
the other stars. I have to look for the stars.

I felt uneasy inside, but I couldn't put the diary
down. All of a sudden, I knew how much I could
like Mary. It was as if just beginning to understand
somebody makes you like them. So Leslie was her
daughter, and the little boy was Timmy. What had
happened to them? I flipped through some pages and
stopped in February.

FEBRUARY 15

I walk through the house crying. It seems all I can do
these days. Leslie is always hugging me. She looks at
me with such sad eyes. I truly think they would be better
off without me. Ted is good to the children. They laugh
a lot together. It's me. It was bad with Ted again last
night. I don't think the kids heard. I closed their doors
once I realized what was going to happen. Had a PTA
meeting this afternoon. They make me so nervous. I was
glad to get home. I even baked a coffee cake, first time
in months. Ted had it for breakfast this morning. He
was so sorry. Said how sorry he was.

What was he sorry for? I wondered. What was
she talking about? And why had she closed the
children's doors? Maybe they fought a lot. Maybe
her husband was angry because she cried so much.

MARCH 9

I can feel spring in the air today. The way the air smells.
The way the wind comes from a different direction. It's
lighter in the evenings. This always made me feel a kind

of joy before. I don't know what's wrong with me. The doctor taped my ribs. He said one was fractured. Ted called twice to see how I was. I told the doctor I tripped on the torn carpet on the stairs and fell halfway down. I think something's wrong with my wrist too, but I didn't want to bother the doctor with that. It seems better already. Timmy is making Easter baskets in school. He had glue in his hair. He says he wants to be a policeman like Daddy when he grows up. He grows so fast. I want to keep him little. Leslie had a fever last night.

The wind had begun to howl outside and whistle through the bare cherry tree. Downstairs I could hear Carol Burnett laughing. I was walking through Mary's life, and I was quiet, as if she might hear me breathing.

JUNE 18

Took the kids to the beach today. Leslie wanted to know why I wouldn't put my bathing suit on. I couldn't tell her. My shift covered everything. Leslie is so sensitive. The slightest thing on me and she has to see it, know about it. Maybe she will be a nurse, too. She said she wants to be the governor and send bad policemen to prison to break rocks. Ted forgot my birthday again. But his mother remembered. She made me a nice cake and gave me another pair of slippers. Leslie was upset she didn't have anything for me. She made me a card when she got home.

There was a small index card decorated with rainbows and flowers and balloons. It was folded and inside it said, "I love you, Mommy. My present is three table sets, five teeth brushings, the garbage out, and seven million hugs. I love you, Mommy. Love, Leslie.''

I was feeling so sentimental and choked up inside, I couldn't stand it. So where was Leslie now? Had she died? And Timmy? And Mary's husband, Ted? Where was he? I turned to the back of the diary to the latest entry. The handwriting was no longer so exact. It was bigger, and the letters seemed to push into each other.

NOVEMBER 7

Job's working out all right. I think my supervisor is beginning to trust me a little more now after I handled the Cunningham child so well yesterday. The child reminds me of Leslie. Today is Leslie's birthday. I am so tempted to call. I ache inside for her. I would give my life to hold my children in my arms again. I can remember their voices, their faces, their softness. But I can't. I have to keep telling myself that. It's so tempting to take a ride and pass the house. Maybe Leslie would come home from school and I could watch her. Maybe I could see her in a store and reach out and touch her and she wouldn't notice. Maybe I could see Timmy play ball down at the field. But no. I'm torturing myself. I can't see Ted. The kids are in good hands. I know how his mother loves them. I know she holds them and loves them the way I wish I could. Sweet Leslie, my lovely darling daughter, happy birthday, my dearest.

By this time I was bawling, just sitting there sobbing, and I knew I wanted to help Mary. So her children were alive, and living somewhere. I wanted to make her all better. I wanted to bring her back to her children. She loved them so much, I didn't understand why she had left them. Page after page was full of little anecdotes about the kids. I looked for the day she moved in with us.

NOVEMBER 1

I am settled now. And holding myself together pretty well. Janet Lewis seems nice, very open and warm, and her daughter reminds me a bit of Leslie. It's nice to be around a child, although she's older, maybe fourteen or so. She has breasts. It makes me sad. I wonder when Leslie will begin to develop. Will Ted's mother help her? The room is pleasant. I sit here and try to feel life. I try to get some joy from the morning sun shining in on the floor. I try to feel warmth, hope, even pain. I feel nothing. I feel tired. When work is over, I sleep. I can hear Janet laughing with her daughter and I want to smash them both. I'm losing it. I hate this ragged crying. I wish someone would hold me, or touch me. I'm losing it. Leslie. Timmy.

I was starting to shiver and I didn't want to read anymore. I closed the journal and put the clasp back on. I carefully pushed it back to the corner of the desk, feeling all spooky and uneasy. I was sorry I had ever looked, because now there was no turning back.

5

When Mary came home at lunchtime a couple of days later, I was sitting at the kitchen table with my orders and catalogues. All the neighbors had been predictably polite, but I had been encouraged by the student council to get a total order of at least three hundred dollars, and polite doesn't do it. So far I had a stupendous order of seventy-three dollars, and couldn't think of another soul I hadn't already hit. Except, of course, Mary.

"Hello, Robin," she said in her quiet voice, and I could tell by the way she looked at me that she intended just to duck her head and walk on by without stopping.

"Got a minute?" I asked.

She stopped and gave me an owl's look. "Sure."

"My school sells holiday junk to raise money," I began, running my hands over the glossy books in front of me. "And I was wondering if you might be planning to send out Christmas cards this year, or give anyone presents. . . ." That sounded stupid. "I mean, would you be interested in seeing what I have, that is, unless you've already bought all your gift wrap already." I was sounding stupider by the minute. And I was having this awful feeling that if she stayed in the kitchen with me, I might blurt out everything I knew, and maybe even cry, and say something about Leslie and Timmy.

She slid her bag off her shoulder very slowly and

placed it on the table. Her white shoes and stockings and her white dress under her coat seemed so official and in charge, but her hand on the catalogues looked like a child's. "Let me see," she said, and she slid into the chair next to me and began thumbing through one of the books.

I watched her as her eyes lingered on the Santa wrap, big Santa faces alternated with drums and dolls and old-fashioned tricycles. She went on to the holly wrap, the red and green ribbons and pompoms, the decorative tape, the clusters of plastic pine and pine cones. "Such nice things," she said softly. I didn't know if she was being polite or just had lousy taste. "Do I have to pay now, or when the order is delivered?"

She looked up at me, and I was startled by how deep her eyes were; they seemed to penetrate right into my head. I looked down at the pictures to hide the shame I was sure she could see. "I'd like a dollar deposit, that's all," I said. "The rest you can pay later."

"And what do you get if you place the biggest order?" Only a mother could have known to ask such a thing.

"Well, the biggest order gets two tickets to the next rock concert at the coliseum, and everyone who makes the three-hundred-dollar mark gets to go out for a pizza with Mr. Kiley, our history teacher." I looked at her and smiled. "Big deal, right? Three hundred dollars for a slice of pizza."

She smiled back at me, and I noticed her front teeth were all capped. I thought only rich people had capped teeth like that. If I hadn't read her diary I would have gone off on another tangent about heiresses and newscasters, but I knew better. "You look a lot like your mother," she said unexpectedly.

"People say that, unless they know my father. Then they know I look just like him."

"Where *is* your father?" she asked, her eyes suddenly lowered to the catalogue in her hand. "I never see him." This was a switch. Was she wondering about me?

"He lives in the city," I told her. "He teaches at the university. They're divorced, my parents. Two and a half years now." I remembered how he had moved out in the spring, the worst possible time, like in that old song—if ever I should leave you.

"Has it been hard for you?" she asked. "Having divorced parents?"

"Yeah," I admitted. "I don't like it." The kitchen was warm and cozy, and I felt myself trusting her. I uncrossed my arms and slipped one over the back of my chair. "How about you? Are you divorced?"

"No," she answered, looking me straight in the eyes. "I've never been married. An old maid, I guess." I would have believed her, she looked that honest and open. Her eyes were clear.

"Ma says there are no old maids anymore. Just women who choose careers instead of families. There are more choices today." I was like a cat waiting for a mouse to come running from under a chair.

"How about you?" she asked. "What are your choices?"

My wheels were spinning. "Well, I'm not exactly sure. I don't know about getting married, but I know I'd like to have kids. Maybe I'd adopt some and not have to be married. Why don't you adopt a kid? Don't you like children?"

"Oh, sure," she said, "I love kids. I work with them at the hospital. I'm a pediatric nurse." As if that took care of it all. "But what about a father for your adopted kids?" she asked. "Wouldn't you feel they were missing something if they didn't have a father?"

"Nah. What they don't know, they won't miss," I said. "It's the missing that's so hard, once you know somebody."

She had put down the catalogues and was studying me closely. "Which do you think is worse? When you only see a parent now and then— Do you see your father?"

I nodded. I knew what she was getting at.

"Or to never see them again? I mean, would it be easier if a parent died, or easier if a parent just moved to the next town and you saw them once in a while?"

"I don't know. I get really sad sometimes," I told her, "when I think of my father alone in his apartment, especially on holidays. But I'm glad he didn't die, I guess." I remembered that one night, early on, when Dad first left, and he and Ma were still fighting over some stuff. Ma was crying, and she told me it would have been easier if he had just been hit by a truck. A day later she took it all back, but I knew what she meant. A friend of mine had her father die of cancer when I was in fourth grade, and when you went to her house, you could tell there was still a lot of love for him even though he was gone. There wasn't anything like that in my house. The only picture of him was in my room, and my mother had really changed stuff around after he left, as if to erase him from our lives.

We both heard Ma's car pull in the driveway outside the window, and it changed the whole atmosphere. It was as if we'd been sneaking something. Talking about private things without my mother being there. Mary opened the catalogue to the last page and pointed to a wreath. "I'll have that," she said.

"Are you sure?" I asked. "It's twenty-five dollars."

"Sure I'm sure. We've got to get you at least to the pizza parlor, if not to the rock concert." She was smiling and kind of phony all of a sudden as the back door opened and Ma walked in. I busied myself with filling in the order, and Mary stood and slipped her wallet out of her bag. I saw something fall on the floor, and without looking I slipped my foot over it. Ma and Mary talked about Christmas shopping and how Christmas always came before you were ready for it, and then I gave Mary her receipt. She told us she was exhausted, and then she went upstairs to sleep.

Ma said, "Isn't she nice?" and "Isn't this working out well?"

"It sure is," I answered, and I retrieved a little plastic card from under my foot and slid it in my pocket. Safe in the bathroom, I pulled it out and read it. It was a Willowtown library card. "Mary Ellen Walker, 24 Dubbin Lane, Willowtown, New York." I memorized it, and later when I put the garbage out, I slipped it into the front seat of her car, so she would think that was exactly where she had lost it.

6

I carried that address around in my head all week long. I knew it would be important, but I wasn't sure how. I wasn't sure what I was going to do with it. All I knew was that Leslie and Timmy probably lived at 24 Dubbin Lane, in Willowtown, and I would have bet those two rock concert tickets that they were missing their mother something awful.

When I went to visit my father, I brought my catalogues and order forms along, thinking I might even ring some doorbells in his apartment house, although he hadn't let me do that last year. "This is not the suburbs," he had said. "People don't like to open their doors, and they're not crazy about kids selling things either."

This time my father had a bad cold, which is when he's at his worst. He's like an old lady. Every hour on the hour, he would fix himself a little tea with honey and take two vitamin C capsules. He settled himself on his big comfortable sofa with an afghan tucked around his legs, and he went over the catalogues so slowly, as if he were selecting instruments for a field expedition to the tundra.

"Who do you buy gifts for?" I wanted to know.

He blew his nose and sighed. "Well, there's you, and Uncle Harry and Bitsy, and their kids. I have dinner with them Christmas day, and then there's

my secretary, and the superintendent of the building, and I usually send something out to Vera and
Nick."

"What do you get your secretary? Flowers? Per-
fume?"

He looked at me over the tops of his glasses.
"Actually, I was thinking of getting him some ski
gloves."

"Him?" I sat up and stared at him.

"Yes, him." He ruffled the papers and continued
to peruse the wraps. "Hmph. For someone who's
being raised by such a wide-minded feminist, I'm
surprised the word secretary has such immediate
connotations of the female sex to you." He was
smirking.

"No kidding? You really have a man secretary?"

"That's right. A nice guy, too. Working his way
through graduate school. He has a serious interest
in paleoclimatology, the study of ancient climates.
Men can work their way up by typing and filing,
too. The world is everyone's oyster now, woman-
child."

There was an edge to his voice. It was what I
expected, him being sick and all. "What are we
going to do today?" I asked to change the subject.

"I have a fever," he told me, pressing his fingers
into his eyes. "I think I'll just stay put and try to
get rid of this by Monday. I've got papers to grade,
department reports to get out. . . ." He looked gray
and tired. "Why don't we just stay here and watch
the hockey game, and then you can run out and
get Chinese food at dinnertime?"

"Okay. But is there anything I could do? I mean
it's only noon, and I don't like hockey."

"Did you bring homework?" Forever practical.

"I don't have any over the weekend."

He sniffed and reached for the box of tissues. This was going to be a real fun day.

"How about I clean out your kitchen cabinets and rearrange them more efficiently?"

"I did that last week," he said, but he was probably lying. He doesn't always like my idea of efficiency.

"How about I rearrange the furniture in your bedroom?"

"Robin," he whined. "Leave my furniture alone."

"Your linen closet! How about I put in that shelving paper that you bought a long time ago and never got around to."

"Okay," he said. "That would be good. Just don't go refolding anything. The way I have it now is just perfect and everything fits."

I stood and slipped my sneakers off my feet. "Don't worry," I promised. "Everything will be exactly like it is now, only the shelves will be lined. You'll see."

By the time we had our shrimp chow mein and moo shu pork my father could barely keep his eyes open and it was only six thirty. He was beginning to cough and wheeze, and I set up the vaporizer for him in his room.

"I'm sorry, Bird," he said, dragging himself off to his bedroom. "I guess this day was really dull for you." He stopped at the linen closet and peeked in. "Ah, very nice, sweetie. You did a good job. See you in the morning." And he disappeared into his room and closed the door. He didn't even remember to pull out my foldaway bed.

I sat in his living room for a while and thought. There was nothing for me to do except watch TV, and I was suddenly lonely for my own bed, and my own refrigerator. I took a piece of paper from his phone message box and left a note.

"Dear Dad, I hope you feel better. I decided to go home and let you rest in peace. Don't worry. I'll take a cab to the station and call you in the morning. Have a good rest and get better." I put a dozen kisses at the bottom and signed my name.

The trip home was uneventful. I had never traveled alone that late on the train, but I kept telling myself it was only seven o'clock, and had it been summer it still would have been light. Winter tricks you like that all the time, making you think you should be tucked in safe somewhere when the night is still young. I was relieved finally to arrive at the station in my town. The old-fashioned lights on the platform glowed with a kind of mist. It was warm for November, and a light fog had settled over everything. It was beautiful, and I decided to walk home instead of calling Ma. It was only a mile, and I like to walk at night.

I started thinking about Mary and her kids. I was sure Mary would never talk to me about them; she had lied already about having any children at all. The only truths I could hope to get would be from her journal, although even there, there were some unanswered questions. I guess that was the first time it occurred to me to go to Willowtown and see Leslie and Timmy for myself. It was about eight miles away. I had done five and back once on my bike. Eight couldn't be much harder. I wondered how I could tell Ma about it, without her knowing about me snooping in Mary's drawers. Maybe I could just tell her about finding the library card. I just knew I wanted to see those kids.

There was an unfamiliar Japanese car in my

driveway. I looked in the windows at the dash-
board and wondered if it was the car that had a
voice that reminded you to buckle your seat belt
and take your key. The gravel crunched under my
feet as I went up the driveway, and a big moon
shone through the pine tree. I was glad to be home.

The back door was open, and I locked it and
bolted it behind me for the night. "Ma, I'm home!"
I announced, loud and clear. I turned to see Ma
standing in the middle of the kitchen. She was all
dressed up in a silky kind of dress that she usually
saved for holidays or concerts, and she was staring
at me as if I were a burglar who had just broken
down the back door with an axe. "Hey, it's me,
your daughter. Remember?"

She just stood there with her mouth open.

"What's wrong?" I asked, drawing up close to
her. "Boy, you look so pretty. Are you wearing
makeup?" And then I saw him. There was a man
standing in the doorway between the kitchen and
the dining room. He was holding a glass of wine
in his hand like he was in some kind of ad for men's
cologne. He was in a suit, and his hair was a little
wild and curly. We all stood there without saying
a word, and then Ma turned the tables and jumped
all over me.

"How did you get home, young lady?"

I stared her down. "The train."

"At this hour?"

I glanced over at Romeo in the doorway. "It's
only eight o'clock. What's the matter? Did I inter-
rupt something?"

Ma bowed her head, and I could see her trying
to compose herself, to put on her company manners. "It's just that I didn't expect you tonight,
Robin, and you know you shouldn't be riding the

train alone at night. Did your father let you leave like this? Why didn't he call me?"

"My father didn't call you," I began, putting guilt and emphasis on each word, "because he's very sick. He's had a fever all day, and he can barely move." I could see past Romeo into the dining room where the table was set with Ma's good china and crystal and, I swear to God, candles. "Not that it matters very much to you. I can see you have other plans. It doesn't matter to you if he's sick or dying." I was barely making any sense, but I was covering my need to bawl. More than anything I guess I was just horribly embarrassed. I could feel my face get hot, and my ears burned.

Ma reached out and touched my arm. "Well, it's okay, Robin. You're here, and you got home safely. That's what counts."

I didn't say a word, and I shrugged my shoulder to avoid her touch. She was just being nice because she didn't want to embarrass herself screaming and yelling at me in front of her date.

"Anyway, I'd like you to meet Tom Mayer. Tom, this is my daughter, Robin."

"I've heard so much about you, Robin," he said, extending his hand to me. What an ass-kisser he was. Heard so much about me. Yeah, he heard I'd be gone for the night, that's what he had heard. I shook his hand and looked down at his shoes, fine leather shoes with no laces or buckles. I could smell him. His hand was warm and felt heavy in my hand. I mumbled something stupid that no one could hear and no one asked me to repeat. I should have stayed at Dad's.

"Robin, would you like to join us for dinner?" Ma asked. "It will be ready in about fifteen minutes."

"Dinner?" I asked, as if I was shocked. "At this hour?" I imitated her reaction to my late train ride. "Thank you, but I ate already with my father." I imagined myself gently feeding my paralyzed father moo shu pork while my mother entertained slick Italian-shoed men in my living room. *My* living room! "If you don't mind," I said, glancing at Tom, "I'll just go up to bed early. I'm tired." He had an amused smile on his face, and he wasn't so good-looking. Boy, for somebody who's hot for Sylvester Stallone, my mother sure did strike out.

"I'd like it if you'd stay," he said. When would he give up? "I was just telling your mother about a promotion tour I was involved in for the group Quiet Riot. Do you know them?"

They were my favorite rock group, so you can imagine the strength this took. "Yeah, I've heard of them," I said. "But I'm tired. It's been a long day." And I walked right past him. "Good night." I wouldn't have cared if he had Prince in his back pocket.

I went upstairs and sat on my bed. I was totally numb. And then I began to get furious. Tell me that having a man for dinner wasn't a secret. I thought we weren't going to have secrets around here. Right. Unless it suits her. Well, I was going to have secrets, too. I waited about ten minutes and then I went back down the back staircase to the kitchen. I shuffled through the phone books and screwdrivers in the cabinet until I found what I was looking for—a map of the surrounding towns— and then I went upstairs. Maybe it was too late for some families to pull themselves together, but it wasn't too late for everyone. Mary didn't seem to have any boyfriends or dates, and if I could just spend a little time with this Leslie, I knew we could work something out.

With a yellow marker pen, I plotted my bicycle trip, and with a string I measured how far it was. Seven and a half miles. No sweat.

7

I was wiped out by the time I got to Willow-town. It was pretty cold out, which isn't too bad for bike riding, but the wind was against me all the way. I kept telling myself that on the way home it would be better. The wind would push me back. I had told Ma that I'd be out for a few hours selling my Christmas stuff, and she didn't ask any questions. Things had been tense in the house all week after me walking in on her little date, and we were pretty much staying out of each other's way.

I had drawn a small map to take with me, and it wasn't till I made my last turn that it occurred to me that Leslie might not even be there. It was a Saturday, but that was no guarantee.

There were about ten kids playing street hockey, so I didn't want to be too obvious and go right to Leslie's house. I went to the corner house, 6 Dubbin Lane, leaned my bike against the stoop, and knocked. No one answered. I walked my bike on to the next house, number 12, and I swear to God, I sold seventeen dollars worth of decorative tape to an old man there, who told me he was going to use the tape on all his gifts and cards that year. What a character. His living room was full of photos of grandchildren and nieces and cousins and other assorted relatives. He was very talkative, and I have to admit I took advantage of this. "A lot of kids on this block?" I asked casually.

"Oh, yes," he said, scratching his yellow-white whiskers. "There are the Bensons next door, four of them, the Rinaldis down two houses, six of them, and then the Walkers." I could see his face grow thoughtful. "There are only two of those children, and it's a good thing."

"What do you mean?" The catalogue slipped from my lap.

"Their mother disappeared. You know, one of those runaway mothers you hear about on the news. What a shame. And such a nice family. Husband's a cop, hard worker. You see him every morning coming home from his shift. Tsk. Tsk. Tsk. So sad."

"Who takes care of the children?" I asked, still as cool as you please. "Are they old enough to stay alone?"

"No, and the boy is a rip. A terror. They really have their hands full down there. The grandmother just moved in with them a couple of weeks ago, and not bad for an old lady, if I do say so myself." He laughed and slapped his leg. "If you stop there, you tell her that old Mr. Hannigan up the block would be delighted to take her to Bingo one Thursday night." He actually cackled.

I got up to leave. What a squirmy old dude he was. I wanted to move on. "Well, thank you, Mr. Hannigan, and I'll deliver your order in two weeks, in plenty of time for your wrappings." It hadn't occurred to me till then that I was going to have to deliver all this stuff when it finally arrived. The thought made me cringe. In two weeks I'd be doing the fifteen miles again, halfway with full baskets.

A fat woman was home in the next house, and she invited me right in, without any hesitation. She was a talker, too.

"I wish I could do *all* my shopping from my living room sofa," she said. She laughed a kind of fat, rolling laugh, and then yelled out at the kids who were playing street hockey. "Larry, you watch that now. I don't want any more trouble, you hear? You're asking for it." Then she said, real slow and threatening, "Timmy. I'm watching you." I looked back out the door at the kids. They weren't paying any attention to this lady. Larry. Timmy. No one looked at her. They just went on playing as if she hadn't yelled a single word.

"What a crew," she sighed, guiding me over to the sofa. "I wish I had a quarter for every black eye on this block." She shook her head, but she was smiling, and I could tell she thought she had a real way with kids. "Can I get you a soda?"

"No, thank you," I said.

"You mind if I have one?"

"No. I'll get my catalogues and order forms ready."

"Confident, aren't you? I like that." She rolled off into the kitchen, and I stood and looked out the window, searching for Timmy's face as I knew it from the photo. Most of the kids had tight helmets on and knee pads. I couldn't see their faces. But suddenly one of the kids started yelling, "Walker, Walker, foul! Foul! Get out!"

I saw a boy freeze there like a wild animal. He was rigid; his helmet was crooked on his head and his arms were bare and coatless even though it was cold out. He held the hockey stick across him and suddenly, in an explosion of fury, he hurled the stick through the air at one of the other boys. The kid lurched away from it, and the stick hit the concrete, broke, and flew off into three different directions.

"Fuck you, McGuire!" he screamed. "Just fuck buck you, you big asshole!" I watched in amazement as this little kid, who I knew was only seven years old, carried on like a maniac. The other kids just stood there watching. A car came down the street, and they moved off. Timmy stormed off in the direction of the house next door and disappeared from my sight just as the fat woman put a tray of cookies down on the coffee table.

"Watching the show?" she asked, looking over my shoulder.

I shook my head. "Wow, that Timmy kid is one hot number, isn't he? What's his problem?"

"No mother," she said simply. She pointed to the dish of cookies, and I took one.

"What'd she do, die or something?"

"Worse. She just disappeared. Packed her bags and took off. Imagine that. I'm telling you, this woman's lib has given more women the craziest ideas. They think it's going to be so great out there, so easy and glamorous. Ha! It ain't so." She took a long swig of soda right out of the half-gallon bottle. "And she had it good. A fine hard-working husband, a nice house. But some women, if they don't get flowers every week, or if they can't have everything they want, they think they can just walk away from their babies and start all over again."

A small boy burst in the front door. He was holding the broken hockey stick in front of him and under his tough helmet and soot-blackened eyes he was crying like a baby. "Look what Timmy did! Look what he did! I'll kill him!"

The fat woman pulled the little boy to her and

in one motion pushed his helmet off his head and ran her fingers through his hair. "Come on now, Larry. Hockey players don't cry, right? You got other sticks. That's enough."

The kid leaned on her fat legs and glared at me. "I'll kill him."

"Yes, yes," she crooned. "Here. Have a cookie."

"Who's that?" he asked as he stuffed a cookie in his mouth.

"This is a girl who's come to sell me Christmas wrapping paper and Christmas cards and ribbon."

"Christmas?" His head whipped around to stare at her. "Christmas? Yeah? You're getting ready for Christmas already? Can I get a new stick? Huh? Can I?"

She laughed and pushed him away from her. "We'll see. Now have another cookie and take off, buster. I got important decisions to make here, you hear me? Scoot. Get lost."

The kid left the broken stick on the floor and ran back out the door.

I hadn't really expected to sell much in Willowtown, but already I was worried about whether or not all this wrap and boxes of cards were going to fit in my bicycle baskets when the time came to deliver. I knocked at number 24 Dubbin, my true destination, thinking how insane all this would have been if nobody was home after all. I waited. There was no car in the driveway. It was quiet. All I had learned so far was that Mary's neighbors thought Mary had had it pretty good, and she had made a big mistake by leaving. But I knew Mary was hardly leading a glamorous life in the rented room at my house. And I also knew from her journal that it had been a painful decision, and she hadn't just taken off on the spur of the moment.

I could hear a shuffling inside the door, and I had the feeling someone was standing right opposite me, behind the thick wooden door. "Anybody home?" I tried. The doorknob jiggled, not as if someone was trying to turn it, but as if a hand had just been placed on it. "Hello," I said quietly, my mouth right near the crack. It opened slightly, and there, a head below me, were two big eyes. It was a girl. Leslie.

"Hi, I'm selling Christmas wrap and cards for my high school."

Nothing.

"Any grown-ups home, little girl?"

Her eyes blinked once, very slowly, like a shade being pulled once down and then up again.

"Your parents? Are they around?" It suddenly terrified me that I might be alone with her. I really hadn't given that possibility much thought. First I just wanted to see where she lived and see what her situation was. Then, I was going to make some kind of plan about approaching her and talking to her.

"Daddy's at work," she said. Her voice was deep and gravelly, like she had a cold.

"Well, how about your grandmother? Mr. Hannigan says your grandmother's here." I opened my case as if in explanation. "I'd like to show her these . . ." I looked up in time to see her eyes do their slow blink again, and I stared at her. Then the door opened wide and an older woman wearing an apron was standing behind her.

If ever there was a perfect grandmother, old Mrs. Walker was it. She was round, and old, and dusted with flour and cinnamon, and she had a silver net in her hair, and an old ring on her finger with tiny black stones in little squares. "Who's this, Leslie, honey?" she asked, her fingers wrapping gently along the side of the child's skinny neck.

"Somebody from the high school," Leslie said. She backed up against her grandmother, expressionless.

Old Mrs. Walker looked at me patiently.

"I'm selling Christmas wrap and cards for my class at school," I began. "And it's a lot cheaper than if you bought them at the store, and we have some really nice designs and colors for all kinds of holiday gifts and greetings."

She didn't say anything. She just stood there as if she were trying to remember something.

"Can I show them to you? Can I come in and show you?"

She stepped aside without a word and I entered Mary Walker's house. I expected it to smell like bubbles, but it didn't. It smelled like cookies and maple syrup. I was aware of looking around, of memorizing things so that if I ever decided to tell Mary where I had been, I would be able to describe everything. The living room was bright, with white walls and red curtains. Around the door plates and at the archway to the dining room there were finger smudges. In the middle of the room, on a large braided rug, was a hockey helmet. There were ivy plants, and in the corner of the room was a TV, pumping out helter-skelter cartoons and noise.

"Come to the kitchen," Mrs. Walker said, and I followed her through the living room and down a short hall that opened into a kitchen. The timer was ticking, and spread on the table, with some cookie trays and a rolling pin, were a math book and several sheets of crumpled paper. "I have to watch the cookies," she said. "And Leslie must finish her homework. What's your name?" she asked abruptly.

"R-r-robin." I stuttered, because I hadn't even thought about that. Should I use my real name, or make one up? "Robin Lewis." It was decided for me.

"What a nice name. Isn't that a nice name, Leslie? Robin. Like a bird. Do you like to sing, Robin?"

I laughed. She actually waited for an answer. "Yeah, sometimes." She opened the oven door and slid out a tray of star-shaped cookies, and slid in a tray of moon-shaped ones. Leslie stood motionless next to the sink, watching me. I smiled at her. Nothing.

"Would you like to see some of the stuff?" I asked Leslie. I wanted her to trust me, to like me. I held out one of the catalogues to her and she plopped it on the drainboard of the sink and continued staring at me.

"All right now," Mrs. Walker said, lowering herself into a chair next to me. "Let me see what you have. I haven't even thought about Christmas yet." She pushed her glasses up close to her eyes and looked down her nose.

"These are the wrappings," I told her, "and the cards and other things are in the back."

The phone on the wall rang and Leslie moved faster than I had thought possible. In one dive she was at the phone and the receiver was to her ear. "Mommy?" she said.

I felt awful, like someone had suddenly shot a hockey puck at my throat. I couldn't look at either of them. I actually bit my tongue. I knew I couldn't say, "I know where your mommy is. I'll get her for you." Not yet, anyway. I couldn't do that yet.

"Gram, it's Daddy. It's for you," Leslie said, holding out the phone in her hand, and when her grandmother took it she sat in her grandmother's seat and stared at the catalogue.

"Sounds like you're waiting for your mom to call," I ventured. I wanted to reach out and tuck her straggly hair behind her ear, like Ma does to me sometimes. I kept my hands in my lap.

Leslie squinted at me. "She'll call," she said, daring me to cross her.

"Your mom work?"

"She's on vacation."

I was surprised. "Oh, yeah? Where'd she go? Someplace warm? Or did she go skiing?" I was beginning to feel confident, as if my smiles and manners were winning this kid's confidence.

Leslie knotted her fingers together tightly, cruelly. "I don't know. Maybe she went to Florida to see her uncle, or maybe to Denver to see her sister, or maybe my father murdered her and put her in the morgue at work."

Jesus. What do you say to that? I just stared at her.

She stared back and then, as if I had caught her saying something really foolish, she shrugged and smiled sheepishly. "Probably she's in Denver," she said.

"Yeah. Probably Denver," I agreed. What I really wanted to do was to put my arm around her and say, "Hey, kid, get your bike and come to my house. I have a surprise for you and you're really going to like it."

Old Mrs. Walker placed an order with me when

she got off the phone with her son. Leslie disappeared while I wrote it up, and when I was leaving I saw her lying in front of the TV, blank-faced and dull, stroking her eyelashes over and over again with one finger. She was breaking my heart.

8

I turned in my order forms the next Monday. One hundred and seventy-five dollars. Too bad there wasn't a prize for the order from the farthest distance. Willowtown. Although I probably couldn't have gotten that either, I remembered, because this girl, Hillary, had grandparents in Port Richie, Florida, and each year they passed the catalogues around to all their old fogy friends. And on top of that, they even paid the postage for all that stuff to go down to Florida.

When I got home from school, there was a note from Ma. "Robin. There's egg salad and tuna. I've got to run to the city for a meeting. I'll call you around 7. Take care of stuff. Thanks. M." I tried to think what Ma had said Mary's hours were this week. Was it three to midnight again? Or midnight to nine? Or hadn't she said something about overtime, and some little kid with bone cancer that she was sitting with? I couldn't remember, but the quietness of the house deceived me, and I ran upstairs, forgetting to bolt the door, forgetting to be cautious.

The door was open a crack and I knocked. "Mary? You home?" I pushed it in and looked around. The room was dark and empty. The shades were still drawn, and as usual everything was neat and tidy, as if no one lived there at all. Two slippers peeked out from beneath her bed, and a pair of glasses glared at me from her pillow. I wanted to read the diary some more, now that I had seen Leslie and Timmy.

I went for the desk, rolling it up quietly, and this time the diary was right in the center inside. The bolt was not clasped, and a pen was lying beside it as if she had just written in it that morning.

I took it out to the hall again and snapped on the hall light. Now I knew Leslie. And Timmy. And the kind grandmother who didn't forget Mary's birthday last June. I looked toward the beginning and sat on the floor with my legs curled under me.

JANUARY 27

Maybe it's something I'm eating. I don't know. I guess I'm drinking too much coffee again. I should be able to sleep when I'm alone in my bed. But I lie awake tossing. When he's there I don't get any sleep, and when he's not, it's just as bad. I'm a nervous wreck. Maybe I can get someone at the hospital to prescribe something. Although I hate to do that. It's bad enough with Ted. . . . And the snow doesn't help. It's impossible to get around. Ted needed his uniforms from the cleaner and I never got over there yesterday. That was his excuse this time. I thought the kids were sleeping, but I guess Timmy had been in the den. When I finally saw him, he was hiding under the desk. God, this is all so sick. I hate for them to see this.

To see what? And why would Timmy hide under the desk? I had seen my parents fight plenty of times, and sure, I didn't like it, and I used to go to my room and close the door, but I never felt my parents didn't want me to see them fighting, especially my mother. Dad didn't go for it too much, but Mom was all for children knowing what was going on. Her parents never fought, she told me, but I was going to see reality.

So maybe Mary just felt like my father and wanted to keep it quiet. But even so, I could never remember wanting to hide, really *hide* anywhere. I thought of little foul-mouthed Timmy, and I couldn't imagine him cowering anywhere either. It didn't make much sense.

I went on to other pages.

MAY 7

Today was a lovely day, Ted's fortieth birthday. A big one, and I thought he might be a bit depressed about it, but so often he fools me. He was positively radiant, as if forty was a big turning point in his life. I was glad. He took the day off and the kids enjoyed blowing up balloons and putting streamers around. Leslie and I baked his favorite chocolate cake. I don't know what was wrong with her. She kept dropping everything, and by the time we were icing it, she was beside herself. Sometimes I have no patience with her, and she's so closed with me. We had the official party after dinner and everything went well. Got the kids up the usual time and worked a little on the dress pattern I picked up for Leslie. I have so little time these days. Ted went out for a while and when he came back I wasn't sure what to expect, but he was so loving and considerate. I love his up moods. I reminded him of his first birthday when we were just married, how we had a party with all our friends. Haven't seen some of them in ages. I should have another get-together again soon, but then I hesitate. I never know. . . .

Never know what? I wondered. I wished I had seen this Ted. I really wasn't sure about him. Maybe

Mary was just exaggerating about the fighting, and maybe she was difficult to live with, crying and all. And he was a cop, so he was probably a good hard-working guy who wanted to come home to peace and quiet at night, not kids fighting or wives weeping. Never had to worry about kids fighting in *my* house, not with just one of me!

It was getting late, but I couldn't stop reading. Just a few more and then I would get something to eat. I wanted to look in October at that period just before she left. I skipped through.

OCTOBER 18

I called Mercy today and I definitely have the job. I gave them the post office box number and told them I didn't have a phone yet, so I've been a real pest, calling and checking. I really have it. Everything is ready for me to go ahead. I can hardly believe it. Every time I think about it, my stomach sinks. But what else can I do? There's nothing else to do. I try to stay away from Ted. But tonight was bad. I hope I last the next two weeks. He came home early, said he had a stomach virus. Leslie had had a nightmare and I was in her room comforting her when he came home. I was lying beside her rubbing her head and trying to warm her. He was in the doorway, saying I was sick, I was a warped mother, and he pulled me off her bed and downstairs. All the while I'm telling Les it's okay, go to sleep, don't have another nightmare, right? Daddy's just going to push Mommy around for a while. That's all. There's no resisting. I am sore all over. I've got to leave.

Was he hitting her? I didn't want to believe it. I didn't believe a cop would do that. Cops kept people from doing bad things to each other. I guess I was pretty dumb. I guess I just wanted to believe what I wanted to believe, that Mary should go back and try again, and that she belonged with her kids, and that nothing is so awful that you can't sit down and talk about it.

I looked at the latest entry.

NOVEMBER 27

Work has been so busy. Lynnie gets worse with every passing day, and there's nothing I can do. If only she'll make it till Christmas. I feel that would give me some peace. I don't know why. I just don't want to be alone for that day. I'm on duty, and I volunteered for overtime. I know the others have families. I have a crazy idea. I ordered a wreath from Robin last week. Impulsive, I guess. But I've decided to bring it to the house. I'll go late at night, after midnight duty, and when I know Ted is gone and I'll hang it on that hook on the front door. They won't know it's from me, but I can picture their faces when they discover it there, and no one will know where it came from. Maybe Timmy will think it's Santa Claus. Maybe Leslie will guess somehow. I picture their faces. All the time.

I heard the door close downstairs, and I nearly jumped right out of my skin. I heard footsteps through the kitchen, as I jumped up and threw the diary in the desk and slammed the rolltop shut. I heard footsteps coming up the stairs as I ran from the room and accidentally slammed the door shut behind me. Mary and I were in the hall facing each other. My back was to her door. It was pretty obvious, I guess.

For a moment we were silent and then she spoke. "Robin, you weren't in my room, were you?"

"I needed a hanger," I said. I was trembling all over. It was clearly a lie. I knew I would never do it again. Please, God, I will never do it again. Just get me out of this one.

Mary bit her lip and watched me. "A hanger? What's the rush? You could have asked me when I got home."

"I didn't know when you'd be back. I'm sorry. I shouldn't have done it. I'm sorry."

Mary stood blocking my way, and my body was suddenly red hot. I could feel my blood like fire in my arms and legs. I thought I might collapse right there if she didn't move over soon and let me by.

"Robin." Her voice was hard, a mother's voice. "Don't ever do that again. Is that clear?"

"Sure, Mary, sure. I'm really sorry. I am. I wasn't thinking. That used to be my playroom and I don't know, sometimes I just forget, and I realized it once I got in there, but then I thought, well, I need the hanger anyway, and then I heard you coming and I got all mixed up, and—"

"Robin, if I ever suspect you're doing that again, I'll have to tell your mother."

I shifted all my weight to one leg and tried to scowl at her. Scraping and bowing wasn't working; I was going to have to act tough. "I said I was sorry, Mary. I made a mistake. If you have to go running to my mother, go right ahead. I don't care. I said it wouldn't happen again." I moved off and shouldered past her, leaving her standing there. I walked deliberately down each step, faking it. My eyes were closed. My heart was pounding, and every muscle in my body was ringing with fear.

9

I avoided Mary after that. In my mind I would have all these imaginary meetings with her where I would do my tough number about hangers and mistakes and so-what's, and then all of a sudden I'd remember what I'd done, and all my best defenses would just turn to mud, and I'd feel all weepy and awful. My only comfort was that in the end everything would be okay. I was so sure of that. In the end, Mary would thank me, and Leslie would be my friend forever, kind of like a kid sister, and the whole Walker family would say, "Well, it wasn't right what that Robin did, sneaking around like that, but it sure has worked out for the best." And they would invite me to dinners, and I'd take Leslie bike riding with me sometimes, and we'd come back here and I'd show her where her mother had stayed during those sad days when she was with us.

"What are you thinking so hard about?" Dad asked me, and I looked up at him. I had forgotten where I was. I placed my hands flat on his wooden table and stared into my juice. "Nothing much," I tried. I would never be able to tell him what I was thinking of doing. He wasn't at all adventurous, and he'd be the last one to understand.

"Have anything in mind that you might like to do today? The museum? Macy's? The movies?"

"What were you thinking of doing at Macy's?" I asked him. Macy's could be great or unbelievably boring depending on what was on your mind when you got there. I loved the wooden-stepped escalators, and the shiny heavy elevators that must have been a hundred years old.

"Oh, I don't know," he said. "You were saying you needed some gloves, and maybe we could find a hat you'd wear. I hate seeing you bareheaded in this cold weather."

I wrinkled my nose at him. "I know," I said. "But you could use some new towels. Some bright fuchsia would look real nice in there with that pink and black trimmed tile, don't you think? Or black! Do they make black towels? Wouldn't that look great? Against the pink tile and the—"

"Robin," he sighed. "Please. I don't need towels. I really don't. The ones I have are just fine."

"But, Dad, they're green."

He didn't understand at all. "They get me dry, Bird, and that's what counts." Sometimes I could wring his neck. I took more juice and stared out the window at the distant rooftops and not-so-distant neighbors' windows.

"I meant to ask you," he said, "how's it going at home? Are you still worried about your mother dating?"

I looked back at him. I could see my face on his face. His was a little heavier, a little darker, but it was certain that we shared a face between us. He looked concerned, loving, and did I see a little tragedy there? Was he worried about Ma dating, too?

"You remember last time when I left here, when you were sick and I went home on my own?" I turned the juice glass slowly around in my hands.

"Ah, Bird, you're not still angry at me about that, are you? I wasn't myself. I was so sick. I really feel awful that—"

"No, that's not it. When I got home that night, Mom had this guy at the house, Tom something-or-other."

He waited, and his spoon stopped stirring his tea.

"She was having this fancy dinner, you know, with all the good dishes and all, and even candles, and she was all dressed up."

He continued stirring.

"Anyway, it was real embarrassing, walking in on them like that."

"Like what?"

"I don't know, like they didn't expect it, or I didn't expect it, or nobody told me, oh, I don't know. I just didn't like it. He was a real creep." I thought of him saying he worked on that promotional tour. "Probably some kind of theatrical agent who takes all his clients' money and uses it on weird Japanese cars. Like the next thing you know, he's going to give Ma some kind of white mink coat, or a diamond bracelet."

Dad smiled sadly into his swirling tea and lifted it to his face. "Look, Robin." He held the glass out to me. "The universe." I looked down into the mug at the stirred milk and tea that formed a pale brown galaxy swirling in steam. I looked in the mug and then at him, and then back at the tea.

"You have quite an imagination, Dad," I said.

He put the glass down and squeezed my hand. He looked deep into my eyes and smiled. "And so, Bird, have you."

That Monday the orders came in at school, and my deliveries were all set up. I kept the Willowtown stuff hidden in my room because I didn't want Ma asking a bunch of questions I couldn't answer. But there was the problem of Mary's wreath. I had been avoiding her since the day she discovered me coming out of her room, and I was really feeling like just sending the wreath back and forgetting it, except I knew that she intended to put the wreath on the door of her house in Willowtown, and I knew how important that would be.

One night I was sprawled across my bed doing my homework with the radio on, and I heard a knock at my door. "Robin? Can I see you, please?" It was Mary, and I opened the door cautiously.

"Hi, Mary. I was just doing my homework." I pointed to my bed full of books and notebooks. I felt I had to prove to her that I wasn't sitting by my door with a periscope and a hidden microphone.

"Yes, well, I was wondering if my wreath came in yet. I saw the other orders downstairs, and I'd like to have it. I was hoping to bring it in to work for someone this weekend."

Neither of us had smiled at each other, even politely. We were stone-faced and grim. "Sure," I said. "I have it right here." I went to my desk and reached into the shopping bag beside it, digging past the decorative tapes and boxes of cards and wrap for the orders in Willowtown, and I pulled her boxed wreath out gently as if it were delicate eggs. She was still standing just outside my door, and it was almost spiteful how she wouldn't step into my room, as if she were showing some exaggerated respect of privacy.

I handed the box over to her and she opened it. She pulled the tissue paper off and looked at the wreath underneath. It really wasn't too bad. It looked better in person than it had in the catalogue. She touched the pine cones tenderly and fluffed the clusters of baby's breath. She smoothed the strands of red velvet ribbon. "That's nice," she said. I knew she was imagining it on her front door in Willowtown with Leslie and Timmy standing before it all wide-eyed and puzzled. "How much do I owe you?"

"Twenty-four dollars." I tore off her receipt, keeping a carbon copy for myself. She put the box on a chair in the hall and counted the money out of her purse.

When she handed the money to me, she smiled. "Can we begin again, do you think? I think we've both been avoiding each other, and I feel kind of . . . I don't know . . . let's start again, okay? Bygones be bygones and all that?"

She was really a nice person. "I'm sorry about—"

"I know. I know." She brushed me off, snapped her purse shut, and picked up her wreath. "And thanks for the wreath, Robin. I have some special people to give it to, and I know it's going to make them very happy." She turned and disappeared into her room, leaving me standing there. I felt a kind of joy in my chest. I imagined her in the night, stealing up to the house and hanging the wreath on the door. I knew what I had to do. As in a Grimm's fairy tale, I would tell Leslie what sign to look for. And then she would know.

10

Saturday Ma wasn't home when I woke up. She had left me another one of her cryptic notes on the refrigerator next to the picture of Sylvester. "Rob. Xmas shopping. All day. We'll do a restaurant tonight. How about it? M." That was a big load off my mind. I hadn't decided what I was going to tell her about Willowtown. I ate a bagel with cream cheese and drank some juice and some eggnog that was in the refrigerator. I also stuck a banana and a tangerine in my coat pockets. I felt like I was going to the North Pole.

The bare trees were motionless against the gray sky outside the kitchen window, and that was one consolation—no wind. But I knew what that gray sky might mean. I checked the thermometer as I went out the back door—thirty-five degrees—and I paused for a minute on the back steps. "Please don't rain or snow," I said out loud. Then I packed up the saddle baskets on my bike with the orders for Willowtown. "And please hold off on the wind." I tucked black plastic bags around the tops of them, just in case. "And please, no flats or slipped chains." I slid my heavy woollen gloves over my hands, tested my brakes, and started off down the gravel driveway. "And please let Leslie be there," I added, on my way. It felt like the most meaningful day of my life.

It's funny, but the ride wasn't as bad as I had

remembered. My energy carried me on at a steady pace, and I'd never felt so right or sure of anything in my life. I'll always remember that feeling. That feeling of something being so right, that deceptive feeling that makes you plow ahead blindly. So sure.

Old Mr. Hannigan was still in his pajamas and a silky kind of robe when I got there. I have to laugh when I think about him. He invited me in and scurried about making me comfortable and then he ran off to change, in order to "receive me properly," he said. He reminded me of a character from *The Wind in the Willows*. His shades were all drawn and a pot of coffee was bubbling in the kitchen. I felt like I was visiting a woodchuck in his little cave. I wondered if he was lonely living all alone like that, like my father, with no one to share the coffee with, no one to get dressed for. I wondered if my father got dressed on the weekends when I wasn't there, or if he just shuffled around in his leather slippers, wiping the toaster and rinsing his dishes. I thought of calling him later when I got home.

"Well, well, well," said Mr. Hannigan. "Let me see my lovely Christmas tapes now, will you?" I pulled out his order, and he spread them on his dining room table. He looked at them as if they were prehistoric arrowheads, and not just tapes decorated with holly and pine cones and stars. He put a shopping bag that was filled with wrapped presents on the table. They were plainly wrapped with just red or white tissue paper. "I don't have my glasses on," he said. "What does this say?" He held one of the packages close to my face to read the light pencil writing in the corner.

"Betty," I told him.

"Ah, Betty." He rummaged through the rolls of

tape. "Betty is definitely the pine cone type. Yes. Yes." His hands trembled slightly as he pulled a length of tape off the roll and centered it on the gift. It looked nice, it really did, but for some reason I got this terrible aching inside and I thought I was going to cry. It was a terrible loneliness, some terrible stirring because he knew a Betty and he thought she was the pine cone type. I watched as he put another piece of tape crosswise on the box and admired it. I loved him for that instant. It occurred to me to not even bill him, to just leave and not collect.

"Now, young lady, what do I owe you?"

"Ah, nothing. That's okay."

He stared at me. "Nothing. Don't be silly." He pulled a roll of dollars out of his back pocket. They all looked like twenties and the roll was as big as my fist. Now I was staring. He peeled off a twenty and handed it to me. "Keep the change," he ordered. "Get yourself a nice little trinket for Christmas, and come back and see me again next year, do you promise?"

Sure, sure, I told him, and the next thing I knew I was standing on his front stoop, and the door closed behind me. You could never tell anything about people.

The fat lady was home next door, and she didn't remember me. I showed her the order to remind her, and then she was all apologies and let me right in.

"I'm so glad I finally have these cards," she said. "Do you think you could get me another box of them? I forgot all about Larry's coaches and scout leaders, and I always like to send one to the crossing guards, and I'd need about eighteen more, I guess another box."

The thought of a fifteen mile bike ride to deliver a box of cards nearly laid me out. "All the orders are in," I lied. "It would be too late now for me to get you another box." I started pulling her three boxes of cards out of my bag.

"But what's this one?" she asked, reaching past me into my bag and pulling out another box.

"That's Mrs. Walker's order," I said, putting my hand on it, but she pulled it out anyway and looked at it.

She smirked at me. "So I get a preview of what Mrs. Walker is going to send us this year, huh? That is if she sends us a card at all. Probably not. She's not very friendly. I tried to get in there last week, you know, just to see if there was anything I could do to help, just being neighborly, and she was as tight as a clam." She shook her head and handed the box back to me. "Still no sign of that mother. Did I tell you about her?" She leaned toward me, and I could smell old coffee breath and something sharp and not so terrific. I nodded. "Imagine Christmas for those poor kids? No mother. I saw the little girl yesterday out front and I says to her, 'What's Santa Claus bringin' you, honey? Think he'll bring your mama back to you?'"

I couldn't believe she had done that.

"But she just stared at me," she went on. "What a weird kid, with her big eyes, and she's so skinny and pasty-looking. What a pain she must be for her father, and that Timmy! Forget it—"

I wanted to get out of there. I stood and said, "That'll be nine dollars and twenty-five cents, okay?"

She leaned back and looked at me. "Well, all right, all right, hold your horses." She went into the kitchen and came back with nine dollars. "I'll owe you the change. I'm short today." I couldn't believe anything about her. I slipped the dollars into my envelope and comforted myself with the fact that Mr. Hannigan had given me a nice tip. I picked up my bag and headed for the door. She just sat there, thinking how rude I was, I'll bet, and I let myself out.

I was hating this. I was getting so depressed and angry and bent out of shape. I made a slow job of walking my bike over to the Walker house and locked it securely in their driveway. There was a car there this time, and I was breathing deeply, calming myself, and trying to think of Leslie and Timmy in their mother's arms, and Mary back here where she could keep that crazy fat woman away from Leslie. And maybe they could move, start over again somewhere. Have a new beginning.

I rang the Walkers' doorbell. I noticed the heavy nail on the door. Its edges were rounded, it had been painted over so many times. There was no wreath there yet.

The door opened, and because I was expecting Leslie or the grandmother, I was surprised when I saw a man standing there. It was obviously Ted, Mary's husband. He had on dark-blue pants and a light-blue shirt, his uniform, I guessed. I didn't see a gun or a badge. I did see his red-rimmed eyes, eyes tired from a long day at work. "Oh, hi," I said stupidly. He waited. "Is Mrs. Walker home?" I hoped he knew I meant his mother and not his wife.

"What for?" he asked. It was a nosy question, but he asked it nice enough.

"I have her order of Christmas cards and wrapping paper. I told her I'd bring them by today."

"She's over visiting her sister."

My heart sank. I could tell he wasn't going to

let me in. "Oh, I guess she forgot." I stared down at my bag. "But you see, I came all the way from Rockland Acres, and she owes me four dollars for this." I held it out to him.

"No problem," he said reassuringly. "I'll pay you and see that she gets them." He pulled a flat black wallet out of his back pocket. "Four dollars, you say?"

"And thirty-five cents."

He was careful like my father is careful, and I watched his face. He was a nice-looking man, with a gentle kind of face, and a smooth neck that folded slightly over his collar. His features were all soft, and yet his eyes were sharp blue, and he was looking at me. We looked at each other. "What's the matter?" he asked.

"Nothing," I said.

He kind of huffed and counted out the dollars into my hand, and then he counted out the change from a pocketful of coins. "There you go."

I handed him the boxes of cards and the tube of wrapping paper. I felt empty inside. I knew I wouldn't see Leslie now. Nothing was working out as I had planned it. I could have bawled as he closed the door and left me standing there in front of that empty nail.

I trudged down the steps with my empty bag and with tears rolling down my cheeks. A snowflake landed on my bicycle seat. It was kind of like someone was laughing at me, making fun of me. I knelt down and fumbled with my bicycle lock. I couldn't do it with my heavy gloves on and I flung them off and tried again. Suddenly there were two sneakers next to me. "Need any help?" Leslie asked.

She crouched beside me and took the lock and the key from my hand. "I'm good at this," she said, and she slipped the key in, turned it, and smiled at me. "See?"

"Thanks." I sat on the curb of her driveway and slipped the key in my pocket. So I would have a chance after all.

She sat down next to me. "You bring those cards and things to Gram?"

"Yep."

"That's good. Christmas is coming." She shrugged. "We can't find any decorations though. Don't know where Mommy put them before she left. Gram looked all over."

"Your mother will bring a decoration for you," I said. My heart was pounding in my throat. There was no turning back now.

She looked at me and did that crazy blink of hers. "She will?"

"You bet." I pointed to the front door. "Right on that door. See that nail? You'll find a wreath hung there one morning real soon."

"I will?"

"Yep."

"How do you know?"

I wasn't sure what to say to that. I didn't want to lose this. I had to control what was happening very carefully. I took a deep breath and spoke slowly. "I just know, and when that happens, it won't be long before you'll be with your mother again."

Leslie suddenly looked away from me at my bike. She looked at my boots, at my coat. "What are you, some kind of fairy godmother or something?"

I smiled. Yes, maybe I was. I liked that. A fairy godmother in jeans and a ski jacket.

"How do you know that?" she went on. "How do you know I'll find a wreath right there?"

"Because I sold it to her," I said. I pulled my

catalogue out of the bag and I opened it to the picture of the wreath. "See this?" I pointed to it.

"Mmmm."

"That's the one. That's the wreath your mother bought, and she's going to put it on the door for you, to tell you that she loves you, and—"

"I don't believe you."

Then I opened my order book and turned to her mother's order. It said "Mary Walker." I pointed to it, and she took it into her own hands and stared at it.

"That's not my mother's handwriting," she said, handing it back to me.

"Of course not. It's mine. But she gave me the order and she paid for it. She has the wreath right now, and she's planning on bringing it to you."

Leslie stood and brushed off the back of her pants with her hands. "You're full of shit," she said. She walked away from me down the driveway.

"Hey!" I called. I scribbled my name and phone number on the back of her mother's order, and I held it out to her. "Here's my number. You call me when you see that wreath hanging there on the door."

Leslie walked back slowly, never taking her eyes off me. She held out her hand, and without looking at it, she stuffed the receipt in her coat pocket. "I still think you're full of shit," she said.

When I drove off on my bike with the empty bag in the basket, I was a little shaky. But I was so sure I was doing the right thing. I just knew it.

11

*W*ednesday *is our* traditional day for spaghetti and meat sauce, and about once a month Ma remembers it. "I think traditions are so important, Robin," she was saying as she stirred the spaghetti. She held her face over the steaming pot and I knew she was letting the steam tighten her perm up. She had a date that night. She told me. It was out in the open. It's probably why she remembered the spaghetti tradition, too. "I remember when I was little, every Friday night my mother would make fish sticks. God! Were they awful. I used to hate them. Just be thankful I never do that to you, Robin."

I was sitting cross-legged on the chair watching her. Things had gotten a little better between us in the last week or so, but it was mostly because we hadn't mentioned Tom. Until tonight. "So why do you think traditions are so important if you hated fish sticks?" I asked.

She settled in the seat across from me and raked her fingers through her curls to fluff them. "Well, the same thing was repeated so many times, and it was so predictable, that if I close my eyes and think of fish sticks, I can see my kitchen from when I was a kid. I can remember the smell of the house, and the basement with the big old oil burner. I think of fish sticks and I can remember exactly what my dog smelled like."

"Yuk. Your dog smelled like fish sticks?"

"No, but remembering the taste of fish sticks somehow triggers a memory button in my brain and I remember all sorts of smells and sights and sounds."

"What sounds do you remember from your house when you were a kid?" I asked.

She lifted her chin and closed her eyes. Her jaw made a fine outline above her neck, like some kind of ancient fossil. I thought my father had probably liked that about her. "Just a minute," she said. "Let me think of fish sticks intensely." It was quiet in the kitchen. The timer dinged for the spaghetti, but she didn't move. "I hear the TV in the living room. Mickey Mouse Club. Annette Funicello. Jimmy." She began crooning. "M-I-C, see you real soon. K-E-Y, why? Because we LIKE you. M-O-U-S-E." She jumped up and turned off the fire under the pot and poured the spaghetti out into a colander in the sink. "How about you, Robin? What memories do you have? What food do you remember? What sounds?"

I closed my eyes like she had and folded my hands in my lap. I went back into my childhood memories, trying to think of a food. "Bologna rolls," I said right away. "Bologna rolled into a tube with a wooden toothpick holding it in place. That's what I can taste." I remembered my father making them for me on Saturday mornings while I watched cartoons. I could remember him coming down early, before Ma was up, in his corduroy pants and his woollen socks. "And Daddy's gray woollen socks with the red toes," I said out loud. I thought some more. I tried tasting those bologna rolls, real deli bologna. What sound did I remember? Bologna rolls, bologna rolls, tasting bologna rolls, and what did I hear? I could hear the fire horn, the town's fire horn that blew to tell all the volunteer firemen that there was a fire somewhere. It was at night. "The fire horn," I said out loud. "I hear the fire horn, and it's at night, and I'm scared, and Daddy comes in and sits by me in the dark till it stops. And he says, 'It's okay, Bird. It's just the firemen putting out a fire.'"

It was very quiet. I opened my eyes to see Ma sitting across from me. At first I thought she had kept her head over the spaghetti steam too long, because long tears were streaming down her face. And then I realized she was crying.

"What's wrong?" I asked, suddenly back in my kitchen with its own smells and sounds and tastes.

"That's so nice, honey. I don't know. That's just so nice."

"Aw, come on." I hated it when she did this. I went around the table and put my arms around her neck. She rested her chin on my arm and patted me. I didn't understand her. I guessed she probably had a lot of the same memories I had. But I couldn't understand how memories of someone you're divorced from, *want* to be divorced from, can make you cry.

"Oh, dear," she said. "Oh, dear."

"Come on," I said, standing up and patting her shoulders. "Let's have spaghetti. Let's make new memories." I swirled around the kitchen with my arms over my head. I pretended I was a psychic, absorbing vibrations and feeling omens. "I taste spaghetti," I chanted. "I smell sauce." I could hear her laughing, but I went on, stumbling over chairs, swirling, swirling. "I see my mother fluffing her perm over the spaghetti steam." I could go on for-ever. I was a swirling sense machine. I was feeling everything all around me, from all parts of my body. "I can feel the draft by the door here. I can feel my shoe sticking to the sticky part of the floor where I spilled juice this morning."

"Ah-ha!" She laughed. And the phone rang.

I stopped in mid-twirl and pointed to the ceiling. "And I can *hear* the phone ringing." I opened my eyes and answered the phone right beside me. "Greetings, from the land of Houdini. This is your medium speaking."

Ma shook her head and got up to finish putting the spaghetti together. There was silence on the phone. "Hello?" I said, more sanely. I composed myself and stared at the dial, waiting for an answer.

"Hello," said a small, frightened voice. "Is this Robin?"

"Yes, it is." For an instant I didn't know who it was. But then suddenly I knew, and my arms raised with goose bumps.

"This is Leslie Walker."

"Yeah. I know."

"The wreath is here."

I took a long deep breath, and thought fast. "Yes, Leslie, well, I can't talk to you right now. We're just sitting down to dinner. Can I call you with the math assignment later tonight? Will you be home?"

"Math assignment?" she asked.

"Yeah, you know, it's hard right now."

"Somebody there?"

"You got it!" I yelled like a crazy master of ceremonies on a TV contest show. I jumped up and down. I was really getting carried away. I felt all hyper and nuts.

"When will you call me?" she asked.

I remembered Ma said Tom was picking her up

at eight. "How about eight thirty?" I asked. "That will give me time to go over the assignment and see what we're supposed to do exactly." Ma pointed to the bowl of spaghetti she had put on the table, and I nodded.

"No later than that," she said. "Okay?"

"Promise. Listen, give me your number." I wrote it down as she said it slowly and carefully. "I gotta go now," I said. "I'll call you later. 'Bye."

I hung up the phone, but as I turned back to the table I had the feeling Leslie was still holding on to her end of the line. I pictured her in the kitchen there the day she had answered the phone, not with "Hello," but with "Mommy?" I was flying. I couldn't wait for my mother to leave so I could be alone.

I don't think I even chewed my spaghetti. And Ma wanted to talk about memories, and I had to concentrate and be real careful to remember a lot of stuff that starred her. Maybe Ma had been crying because she thought I just had memories about Dad. I told her how I remembered the summer when the therapist told her that instead of spanking me, maybe she could shoot me with a water pistol. Now that's a memory. I can still see her stalking through the neighborhood backyards like a gang-ster, with a water pistol clutched in her hand, out to get me. It worked better than the spankings, too. I guess because we'd end up laughing.

Well, there was one thing I could say about Tom at that point, and that was that he was prompt. While the clock in the hall was bonging eight, I could hear his footsteps coming up the front stoop. The doorbell rang on the eighth bong. Ma was still upstairs, getting dressed. I opened the door as if I was just going to check the weather anyway, and let him in. It was cold out, pretty nippy. My breath rose before my face.

"Well, Robin, what's up?" he asked.

I gave him a split second's worth of eye contact and went into the TV room. "Nothing," I told him, and he followed me in. I switched on the TV and put on the music channel. I stared at the video, ignoring him.

"You like Madonna?" he asked.

"Yeah," I answered. What was he going to do, tell me how he was just on tour with her?

He tossed a cassette tape beside me on the sofa. "Then you might like this. It's a copy of one of her original demos. A friend of mine played it for me. I made a copy."

I picked it up and turned it over in my hands, reading the handwritten labels. Actually it really was pretty neat. I glanced at him. "Thanks." But I guess I was too friendly, because he took that as an invitation to sit down next to me and watch the video.

"Ma!" I yelled. "He's here!"

I heard her muffled answer from somewhere far away, it seemed, and I continued to stare at the tube. He smelled like cologne and I wasn't sure I exactly hated it. His corduroy legs were long on the sofa near me, and the toe of his cowboy boot tapped along with the music. And I swear to God, he was singing the words to the song. Now have you ever known any old person at all who knew the words to a Talking Heads song? I didn't say anything. I didn't want him to know I was impressed. I just balanced the tape on my knee and sat there.

Soon Ma came waltzing down the stairs and

peeked in at us. "Getting to know each other?" she sang.

I rolled my eyes.

"Yes," he answered. "By osmosis. We're absorbing each other's vibes. We're grooving on this tune. We're burning down the house."

I couldn't help it. I laughed.

"Well, come on, Robin," Ma said. "Lock the door after us, and don't wait up. But I shouldn't be late, about eleven or so."

"Okay, okay, Ma."

I walked them to the door. I stepped out on the front porch with the front door open and bright behind me, and I watched them walk out to his car together. He opened the door for her. "Thanks for the tape," I called. He held up his hand in a sort of salute, and then got into his car on the other side. I listened for the voice of the lady saying, Fasten your safety belt, or something, but the night was quiet. I stood there until they were out of sight, and I was shivering. Then I went inside to make my phone call.

Old Mrs. Walker answered. "Hi. Is Leslie there?"

"Yes, just a minute," she answered in a funny sort of official voice, as if I were somebody important or something. I heard her call Leslie.

"Hello?"

"Hi, Leslie. It's me. Robin."

"The wreath is on my door," she said again.

"I know. I told you, didn't I?"

"Do you know where my mother is?" She was whispering.

"Yes, I do. And she misses you very much."

Leslie was quiet for a long while, and I heard her take a deep trembly breath. "Is she coming home?"

"Do you want her to?"

"Yes," she answered. "You tell me where she is, and I'll come get her and bring her back." She made it sound so simple. I guess at that point I believed it was simple, too.

"I'm not quite sure how to work this, Leslie. We have to be careful. I don't know why your mother left you, but she must have had a good reason. I just know that she misses you very much and she's very sad not to be with you and your brother right now. She really missed you on your birthday last month." I was slowly turning around, and the phone cord was winding around me like a corrugated snake, up my calves, my knees, my thighs.

"Did she tell you that?" she asked.

"Sort of. She let me know," I answered.

"She left because of my father. But I think he'll be good now. He's very sad. He'll be good if she comes back. I know it. I heard him crying."

"I'll tell you what, Leslie. Let me find out what your mother's schedule is for the week. She works at a hospital near here. And once I know we'll arrange some kind of meeting where you can talk to her. Just you, though, you understand? Don't tell anybody about this, not your grandmother, your brother, your father, nobody. Okay?"

"Yes." Her voice was so small.

The cord was wrapped around my hips, my waist, my arms. "And I know that once she sees you and has a chance to be with you even for a little while, she'll want to go back with you. I just know it. She's very unhappy."

It sounded like Leslie was crying on the other end.

"Leslie?"

No answer.

"Come on now. Don't be sad. This is going to work out fine. You'll see. Come on. If you cry like that your grandmother will see you."

She sniffed. "Okay. Where can I see her?"

"I'll figure that out," I answered. "Can you ride a bike?"

"Sure."

"I mean, really far? Like seven or eight miles?" I thought about her skinny little legs. Maybe I could ride her on my bike, on the back, and then her mother could drive her home.

"Sure I can. I ride my bike all the time."

"Yeah, but seven miles is far."

" 'S okay. I can do it."

The cord had reached around my shoulders and now my neck. I stood still and stared at the dial. "All right," I said. "I'll think about it. And I'll call tomorrow or Friday, and I'll tell you how we're going to work this."

"Robin?"

"Yeah?"

"You *are* like a fairy godmother, you know that?"

I felt like a million bucks.

"And Robin?"

"Yeah?"

"I'm sorry I said you were full of shit."

"That's okay. Forget it. I would have said the same thing to someone if they had told me what I told you. How does that old wreath look up on your door?"

"Very beautiful," she answered. "It's the most beautiful wreath I ever saw."

We were quiet. There was nothing left to say. "Well, I'll be talking to you," I said. "Tomorrow or the next day."

"Thanks, Robin," she said.

We hung up and I stood there a minute. I saw them all gathered for Christmas, together and happy, loving and full of possibilities. We'd all sing Christmas carols, the Walkers and us. My father plays carols really well on the piano, and we could all sing and have hot mulled cider and decorated cookies. It would be great. I turned around the other way and easily unwound my way out of the phone cord. Some messes are easier to get out of than others.

12

*T*hursday *was a* wasted day in school. I couldn't keep my mind on anything but arranging for Mary and Leslie to get together. My brain was like a lunatic hamster spinning its wheel. I went through every possible idea. At first I thought it would be best if I asked Mary for a favor. I would ask her to drive me to that special candle store in the mall in Willowtown to do Christmas shopping for my mother. And I could tell Leslie to meet us by the Santa there. But then I thought that Mary probably wouldn't want to go near a shopping center in Willowtown, just in case she ran into somebody she knew. She wouldn't agree to that.

I knew that whatever I did, I was going to have to get Leslie to come to Mary. And there were only two ways to do that—either I'd ride Leslie on the back of my bike, which I wasn't too crazy about, or I'd trust what she said, that she was a good bike rider. I could ride to her house right after school, meet her, and then lead her back here. If I left my house right after school, I'd get to her house about four. If she was ready and we left right away, we'd get back here a little before five. I didn't like it. It would be dark, and although I had lights and reflectors on my bike, I didn't like riding in the dark, and Ma would be furious.

And that was another problem—Ma. I really didn't want her in on it. I chewed on this all day, worrying about how I was going to do it. When was Mary going to be at the house? When was Ma going to be gone? I wanted Mary there and Ma out, and I tried to think up a million ways to make it happen, but once I got home I realized things were going to work out just fine by themselves without too much juggling on my part.

Ma was restless and mumbling when she got home from work.

"What's wrong, Ma?"

She hung her coat on the doorknob and stuffed her hat in her pocketbook. "I'm trying to work out my schedule for next week. It's such a bad time of the year to get anything done. Why doesn't Christmas come in February? That's a nice boring month with nothing to do. I should write to my congressman. Who *is* my congressman?"

She didn't even wait for an answer. She just whisked by me and went upstairs to her room. I followed her up and plopped myself across her bed while she changed. "Jerry needs the reports in a week. Martha misplaced the last quarter file, so I have to tear everything apart looking for it. I'm never going to get into the city to do the shopping I wanted to do. And it's just ten days to Christmas." She was slamming drawers and doors and tossing shoes around like a crazy person. I watched in wonder. When she was all done she was standing there in sweat pants and a sweat shirt and sneakers. Her hair was droopy, and she had black smudges under her eyes. She ducked into her bathroom and I could hear her splashing around. "Robin?"

"What?"

"Robin?" She came out and walked over to the bed, wiping her hands on a small towel. Her face was shiny and wet.

"What? What?"

"I have to ask you something," she announced.

"I can tell."

"Would you mind . . ." She got down on her knees beside the bed. "Would you mind terribly, awfully if . . ."

"Spit it out, Ma," I told her. I couldn't imagine what she was trying to say.

"I know I've been late quite a bit lately, and I've had stuff to do while you're here, and you've been alone a lot—"

"I don't mind. It's no problem."

"One more time." She held her folded hands up as if she were praying, a real clown. "One more time. I want to get into Bloomingdale's in the city next week. It'll be another late night, but then never again. Just once more, and I will never leave you again. I swear it."

"Cut it out. So go! Buy me a lot of good stuff. I know that's what you're going to do anyway."

"Oh, you're a dear. No guilt. A guilt-free day at Bloomingdale's, as long as I get you stuff!" She snapped the towel at my leg and went back to the bathroom. "But which day is best for you, Robin? Monday, Tuesday, or Wednesday? I could do it any of those days. Do you have a preference?"

I thought to myself about next week. I knew I wanted Ma to be out on the day I worked my plan. But I didn't know yet which day Mary would be here.

"Tell you what, honey," she went on, without waiting for my answer. "Why don't I ask Mary when she'll be here, and maybe she wouldn't mind fixing a dinner for the two of you. That might be nice, huh?" She peeked around the door.

I couldn't believe it. Normally I wouldn't want

anyone to fix me dinner. I was perfectly capable of getting something together myself, but this was all falling into place for me so easily, as if it was meant to be, as if there were powers beyond my control guiding the entire thing. "Sure, Ma," I answered, trying to sound casual about it. "That would be good. Check with Mary. See what she says." I slid off the bed and twirled in front of my mother's full-length mirror. I had this wild feeling of destiny flowing through my life. Everything was falling into place as if it was all mapped out ahead of time, just waiting for me to set it in motion. I knew Mary would be back with her family for the holidays.

At dinnertime that night, Mary told us she would be off from her shift at work on Monday. She agreed to come home that day and fix dinner for the two of us. Well, the three of us, actually, but she didn't know that yet. What a great day that would be. I couldn't think of anything except what their faces would look like when they first saw each other. Of course, Leslie would know what to expect, but Mary would be totally surprised.

Mary would be at the stove in the kitchen, and she would be thinking about how she missed cooking for her family, and she would turn as the back door opened. She would expect to see me, just me, but there would be her daughter. They would be so happy to see each other, hugging and kissing like some kind of Shirley Temple movie. I would start to leave, and they'd beg me to stay and join them, and we would all eat together, and Mary would plan to go back with Leslie. She would drive her home and stay. I felt shivery inside and weak.

"Finish up here, Robin," Ma said, breaking into my guarded silence. I'd probably been drying the same dish for five minutes. It was squeaking beneath the towel. "*On the Waterfront* is on in five minutes. You *have* to see it."

"I've seen it, Ma, I've seen it."

"You have?" She really looked surprised.

I laughed. "Yes. You made me watch it three times already."

"Not enough," she said.

"How many times is it now for you?" I asked.

She didn't hesitate a second. "This is seventeen."

I shook my head and dried a glass.

"Come on. Come on," she pleaded. "Finish up. Oh, I wish I had time to make popcorn. It'll be on any minute."

"I'll make the popcorn," I told her. "You go ahead. I'll be there in a minute."

"But I don't want you to miss any of it!"

"Ma! I've seen it three times. So I'll miss the part where they throw the guy off the roof. I have to make a phone call anyway. I'll be in when I'm done."

I poured some kernels into the popcorn popper and put a blob of butter in the melter. I plugged it in, set a bowl under the opening, and pulled Leslie's phone number out of my back pocket.

This time Leslie answered right away. "Leslie?"

"Hi, Robin. I was waiting for you." She sounded excited.

"Okay," I said, "I have good news for you. Monday. That's the day."

She didn't say anything.

"Aren't you excited?"

"Yeah, sure, but are you sure she wants to see me?" I couldn't believe she asked that. "Daddy said she left because she doesn't love us. She doesn't care about what happens to us."

"That's not true, Leslie." The skin prickled on the back of my neck and the hair stood up on my arms. How could she even think such a thing? "That's not true at all. Your mother loves and misses you so much. I told you that. It's awful for her without you."

"All right," she said slowly. "What do I do?"

"Well, what do you normally do after school on Monday?" I asked.

"I have band practice at school."

"Let your grandmother think you're going to band practice anyway, okay?"

"Yeah."

"Do you take your bike to school?"

"Sometimes."

"Well, take it Monday, and after school, skip band practice and meet me on your corner by Mr. Hannigan's house. I might be a little late. I'll get there as soon as I can. Just wait there, no matter what."

"All right."

"And dress warm. It's a long trip. You sure you're good on your bike for a long trip?"

"I said I was. Why do you keep asking?"

"I don't know. You just look kind of little. It's seven and a half miles."

"Do I have to ride it back, too?" she asked.

"No. I'm sure your mother will drive you back."

"Will she come back to stay with us?"

"I can't tell you that for sure. I don't know what she'll decide. That'll be between the two of you. You'll know after you see her."

She was quiet and I could hear her breathing against the mouthpiece. I stopped breathing and closed my eyes.

"You're missing one of the best parts!" Ma yelled

from inside. I looked over at the popper and saw that it was blowing out popcorn all over the counter, overflowing the bowl.

"Just a minute!" I yelled back. "Listen, I gotta go," I said to Leslie. I unplugged the popper and began scooping the popcorn into the bowl. It was the first time I noticed my hands were trembling. "Just remember, Monday after school, down by Mr. Hannigan's house. You got it?"

"Monday. Old man Hannigan's house. Got it. See you then."

"Robin!" Ma yelled. "Quick! If you don't see this part, you won't understand later about the bosses and the brother and stuff."

I wanted to strangle my mother. I poured the butter over the overflowing popcorn, picked up the bowl, and headed inside. I left a trail of popcorn through the dining room, like Hansel and Gretel did to help find their way back. But there was no heading back now, and a dull feeling of uneasiness was beginning to stir inside me. It was as if this whole plan was an image in a kaleidoscope that could shift and slip away if I moved it. I was holding on real tight to the "rightness" of the whole thing, trying not to think, trying not to move.

13

I got all dressed up that day to go to school.
I felt like it was sort of a golden day, a turning
point, a milestone, not only in Leslie's life, but
somehow in my own as well. I was flying, but I
couldn't do anything right. My new jeans were too
stiff, I couldn't find my socks with the silver threads
in them, my lavender shirt felt itchy, and I couldn't
get my mascara on without smearing it on my lids.
The day at school was torture. I rushed from class
to class barely speaking to anyone, and in class I
would get through the period by writing the time
on the bottom of my notes. 12:35, 12:40, 12:45,
five minutes at a time, as they passed, willing the
day to pass.

I was the first one to the bicycle rack when the
final bell rang, and I realized I was going to have
to take my school books all the way to Willowtown
and back. I didn't want to take the chance of stopping home and running into Mary. Oh well, I had
carried all my Christmas orders last time. Traffic
was heavy starting out, but I stuck to the side of
the road and kept my head down against the cold
wind. I had remembered my hat, which I pulled
way down over my ears, but my gloves were missing. I hadn't gone a mile and already my fingers
were hurting. I could see the skin crinkling on the
backs of my hands, so I rode one-handed, with the

other hand in my pocket, first my left, then my right.

By the time I got to Willowtown I had pulled my shirt sleeves out from beneath my coat sleeves, and had folded them over my freezing fingers. My legs were like ice under my stiff jeans, and I felt raw.

Leslie was sitting on the curb by Mr. Hannigan's, out of sight of her house. Her bike was on its side under the hedges, and she was tossing pebbles into the street. I pulled up right in front of her, put the ends of my sleeves near my mouth, and huffed on my dead fingers.

"You forget your gloves?" she asked, as if she saw me every day of her life.

"No, I hate gloves. They ruin my image." I was immediately sorry for being sarcastic. "I didn't forget them," I said, softening. "I must've lost them in school. I feel really stupid, and cold." I smiled at her.

Without smiling back or even looking at me, Leslie stood and pulled her bike upright. She rolled it into the street, sat on the seat, and put one gloved hand under her arm. She pulled her hand out and handed the glove to me. "Here," she said. "One's better than nothing."

I wanted to say something reassuring to her, something loving, but my mind wasn't working any better than my fingers were. I took the glove, and on impulse reached out and tucked a wisp of her yellow-white hair neatly inside her hood.

She stared at me blankly. Her eyes closed and opened, and I looked away. She had a way of making me feel like everything in the world was insignificant, everything except her. "Okay, let's go,"

I said, and we pedaled out into the middle of the street and started on our way.

I felt like some kind of caravan leader. I was rescuing this little child who had been kidnapped by bandits. I had been working as a servant in her mother's palace, so I knew all about her. I had watched her play in the luxurious gardens and fountains. I had watched her learn to ride her father's camel. She had called me "Tanta," and we had many happy times together.

I turned and looked back at Leslie. She was pedaling like mad and watching me. She hadn't realized yet that her one hand would be better off in her pocket. There was a grim determination to her face, and her skinny legs pedaled kind of crooked, like she was knock-kneed.

We would find her mother in the royal tent on the way to a festival. Her mother would be so sad, so lonely for her lost child, until she saw me. She would look up, and say, "Oh, Tanta, anything? Any sign of her? Any hope at all?" The mother would dread my answer. Perhaps I had found a piece of her dress torn on a cliff. Perhaps I had found a circle of buzzards. But no. "Madam," I would say, "the news is of the best." And I would stand aside and gaze at the opening to the tent, and the child would enter, ragged and dirty, but when she smiled, doves would flutter about the tent. There would be music, laughter, and the mother and child would run into each other's arms. And the father would step into the tent when he heard the commotion. They would all smile at each other in utter amazement, and then they would whirl in circles about the tent, the three of them, arms locked, cheeks brushing, eyes shining.

We waited at a light, next to each other. Leslie

waited with her foot on the curb and I stood next to her. "How're you doing?" I asked.

"Okay," she answered. She looked at me cautiously. "Does my mother know I'm coming?"

"Not yet. But she'll be at my house."

"Why is she at your house?" she asked.

"We'll tell you later. You'll know the whole story, don't worry." The light changed, and we shoved off.

It wasn't dark yet, but there was a peculiar wintertime light of an early dusk that made everything seem unreal. It made even the dull little neighborhoods somehow noble and holy, and it reminded me of another bike ride I had taken once when I was about six and I had gone with my parents to Holland. We went to the island of Texel on a ferry. When we got there we rented bicycles and rode all over the island. The bikes were the heavy one-speed kind, and although I had just learned to ride a two-wheeler, Dad wouldn't let me ride my own. I straddled a special flat seat on the back of his with my feet carefully placed on little rests on each side of the wheel.

Every road in Texel had an adjacent bicycle path, miles and miles of inlaid brick roads, smooth and wandering. Far from the town where we had rented the bikes, it began to drizzle, fat, wet North Sea drops that made us stop. We sat under an overhang at an abandoned farm building and watched a small grass-roofed house across the way. It sat like a heavy upturned wooden shoe with rain running down its sides. We huddled together, Dad, me, and Ma, with me in the middle, and they had their arms around my shoulders, but I knew their hands went past me to touch each other's backs. And I remembered the light, the pink-gray glow along the edge of the land, and the holiness, the rightness of the three of us being there. I remembered the feel of my breath going in and out of my nose, and I remembered looking at that house, but being able to see my nose and the bones around my eyes. I remembered feeling like once I hadn't even existed, but my parents had, and I had chosen them somehow, and the three of us really made two, or one, or some number that didn't exist except in my mind. I remembered Leslie was behind me, and before I turned to check on her, I wiped the tears off my cheeks with the back of her glove.

She was doing pretty well, and we were more than halfway home. My cold feet kept pushing the pedals, left, right, left, right, and as they did I found myself thinking about what I was doing and saying inside, yes, no, yes, no, possible, impossible, this is right, this is wrong, this is fine, this is crazy. So much was whirling around in my mind, and a peculiar nervousness was starting to rise, an edginess so strong that I began to push with just one foot, letting the other foot rest, saying over and over to myself, left, left, yes, yes, possible, this is right, this is fine, it's okay. Everything is going to be just the way I want it.

When we arrived at my house, I panicked when I realized Mary's car wasn't in its usual spot by the garage. Leslie followed me up the gravel driveway. There weren't any lights on in the house, and my stomach was in a cold knot. But I didn't let on. I showed Leslie where to stand her bike, and I walked casually back toward the house. I think I even whistled.

"Nobody's home," she said.

"It's okay," I lied. "Your mom'll be here in a few minutes."

I snapped on the light at the back door and searched for the key in the clay flower pots. My fingers were so cold I could barely feel the pots, and one slipped through my fingers and cracked in two at my feet. I didn't know if I was trembling from cold or fear. Leslie picked up the two pieces, fitted them together, and stood them back on the shelf while I unlocked the door and stepped inside. It felt warm inside, but there was no smell of food cooking, no noises of a busy kitchen. The phone was ringing.

"Hello?" I shouted, picking it up. I hadn't realized that my ears were frozen, too. I winced.

"Robin? Is that you, dear?" It was Mary. "Where have you been? I've been frantic."

"I had to do something," I said stupidly. "But where are you? Ma said you'd be home tonight. We're supposed to have dinner together." I knew I was whining.

"That's why I'm calling." I heard her cup her hand over the mouthpiece and speak to someone in clipped, short orders. "Hello?"

"Yes," I said, "I'm still here." And where was she, for God's sake?

"We've had an emergency here at the hospital, and I know I promised your mother I'd be there, but—"

"But you have to come home," I pleaded. I thought I was going to cry. Leslie stood next to me with her hat in her hand, and dark black circles under her eyes. I knew those circles weren't the kind that rubbed off.

"Robin, be reasonable. You're perfectly all right there by yourself. I know you can take care of yourself and get a meal together."

"But Mary—"

"I wouldn't do this unless it was an emergency,

and I'll apologize to your mother in the morning, but it doesn't look like I'm going to be able to get home till this shift is over, maybe by eleven or twelve."

"Eleven or twelve! But Mary, you have to come home. You have to."

"Why? What's the matter?" I could hear voices shouting in the background.

How was I going to tell her this? "Well, you just have to. I have an emergency here, kind of, in a way."

"Robin," she said, "what are you talking about? Come on. I have to hurry." She waited for my answer. Suddenly it was deathly quiet on the other end. All I could hear was Leslie's breathing.

"Leslie's here," I said. I felt like I had lit a firecracker, laid it in the grass, and run. Now I could hear the electric whir of our kitchen clock. I think I could even hear the oak table cracking with age.

"What?" Her voice was thin, like a razor blade.

"Leslie is here. She's come to see you. She wants to see you and she's here right now."

"Oh, no. I'll be right there," Mary said, and she hung up the phone and left me alone.

I put the phone back on its cradle and turned to meet Leslie's stare. Her mouth was twisted into a painful shape. "She's not coming," she said.

"Oh, no, no, no!" I said. "She *is* coming! Right now. She had an emergency in the hospital, and she wasn't going to be able to get home to be with me, but when she heard *you* were here, she said immediately, yes, yes, she was coming."

I slipped my coat off, being careful not to break off any of my frozen fingers, and I threw it on the back of my chair. "Take your coat off," I said. "And relax, for God's sake. You look like a scared rabbit. Believe me, it's gonna be good. You're gonna see your mother. It'll be great."

I rubbed my hands together and stood near the radiator. Leslie opened her coat and slid into a chair. She stared straight ahead, and kept her hands hidden in her pockets. I looked down at her sneakers and thought how sad they were with their three beaded friendship pins on the laces. And then I was struck with how awfully sad *she* was, and then like spring mud, sadness seemed to flow all over me, and I was sad, too. My kitchen was sad. The dusty light fixture hanging over us was sad. The empty pots. The partially opened drawer. The chair where my father never sat anymore. *Oh, no,* Mary had said when I had told her. It was all so sad.

"I'll make some hot chocolate," I said, trying to mask what I was feeling and the dark doubts that were rising in me. Why hadn't Mary sounded happy? Didn't she want to be with Leslie? I told myself there was probably just a mess at the hospital, rows and rows of stretchers with injured people, all reaching to her, needing water, a crutch, or medication. She was just busy, that was all.

I scooped out four heaping spoonfuls of chocolate drink mix into each mug and plunked them on the table in front of Leslie. She didn't move. I turned the fire on under the water and sat down beside her. "Well," I said, "well."

Leslie turned her eyes on me and blinked slowly, closed and opened. She fell asleep, she woke up, in a split second. "My mother doesn't want me," she said. It was the last thing I wanted to hear.

14

*J*ust *when the* water in the pot began to boil, I recognized the sound of Mary's tires spinning on the driveway. "There she is now," I said. We waited, and I heard running footsteps coming up the back steps. Goose bumps rose on my arms and down my back, the door flew open, a lump caught in my throat, she burst into the kitchen and stood there, with her coat open and dried caked blood splattered down the front of her nurse's uniform.

She looked at me and I could tell she was in a rage, and then she turned her attention to Leslie. Leslie stood frozen to the spot, gaping at the blood on her mother's dress. Following her daughter's gaze, Mary looked down at herself. She covered over her dress quickly with her coat, as if she were embarrassed, and then she scooped Leslie up in her arms. She sat in the chair with her long-legged daughter in her lap and ran her fingers almost cruelly through the child's hair. "What are you doing here? What are you doing here?" she murmured over and over. Leslie had begun to cry. Her arms wound tightly around her mother's neck and her face was buried in the brown woollen collar.

"Robin got me," she whispered. "I want to bring you home."

"Ah," Mary crooned in her child's ear. "Shh, now. It's all right, now." Our eyes met over Leslie's head. There was blood in her eyes, as clear as the blood on her dress. "Tell me, Robin," she said. "What is this? What's happened?"

I felt trapped, ashamed. This wasn't at all the way it was supposed to be. I felt my face grow hot, my arms tingled. "Families should be together," I blurted out. It was all I could think of to say.

"I think so, too," she whispered, controlled, as if she thought if she raised her voice it would shatter windows. "But why is Leslie here right now?"

"I saw Leslie's picture. I knew you loved Leslie."

Her brow drew together, puzzled. "What are you talking about? I never showed you a picture of Leslie."

"I saw the pictures in your drawer. Of Leslie and Timmy."

"My drawer?" I suddenly knew what it must be like to look down the barrel of a loaded rifle. I wanted to drop to the floor, to get out of range.

"My drawer?" she repeated.

I just nodded.

Leslie hadn't taken her arms from around her mother's neck, and now Mary buried her face in her daughter's hair. I remembered reading in her journal about how she longed to hold her children. Why wasn't she smiling? Why wasn't she thanking me? Without lifting her face to me, her eyes rolled in her head and she stared at me. Slowly, so slowly, I can still remember the weakness that grew greater and greater in my knees and my calf muscles, slowly her head rose up, the stare never leaving the bones of my face. I would turn to ashes from her look and flake to the floor. She wet her dry lips and spoke to me.

She said, "You have ruined everything, you miserable child."

There was no answer. I couldn't believe I had ruined anything, not anything at all. I wanted to shake her and say, "Look! You have your daughter in your lap! Aren't you glad? Have you forgotten how much you wanted her? What kind of a mother are you?" But I just stood there. I realized the water was boiling for the hot chocolate, and I shut it off. When I looked back, Leslie had loosened her grip and was watching her mother's face closely. Mary was looking at me, and I wanted to scream at her. She didn't deserve to have kids. Maybe all the neighbors were right about her.

"How did you find my address?" she asked.

"You dropped your library card one day in the kitchen here. I copied it down." My voice was hard and I was hiding behind it, like I would if a teacher got me backed up against a wall about something. I knew I was going to have to face all this, and I knew now that there was no way I was going to come out of it feeling good.

"You didn't give it back to me," she said.

"I put it in your car." I stared back at her defiantly.

"Why the secrecy? Why the duplicity, Robin?"

I shrugged.

"What else have you done? What else besides the pictures, Robin?"

I didn't move.

"You read my journal, didn't you?"

I nodded.

"I thought so that day when I caught you coming out of my room. The desk looked different somehow, but I thought, 'No, Robin wouldn't do that. Not Robin.' " Now she was mocking me.

"You should be with your—"

"It's none of your business!" she shouted. "None of this was any of your business!"

Leslie began to cry. "Mommy! Mommy! Don't yell. I want you to come home. I *wanted* Robin to come get me. I want you to come home." She was crying in gasps, choking and sobbing, and Mary turned from me and stroked Leslie's head.

"It's all right, now. Shhhh. Don't worry. It's all right." She sat there rocking her child on our wooden kitchen chair. I couldn't move, couldn't think of anything to do, so I just stood there stupidly and waited.

After a while Mary got up and helped Leslie onto her feet. She tugged Leslie into her coat and then zipped it up for her, pulling her hood up and tying it under her chin. Leslie stood there as if she were four years old. Mary did not look at me, but by the harsh tone of her voice I could tell it was me she was talking to. "I want you to wait right here," she began. "I am going to drive back to Willow-town now. Leslie and I are going to talk a little, and then I am going to take her home to her grand-mother."

"Mommy—" Leslie whined, but her mother went on.

"I want you to wait here for me. You are not to leave this house, is that clear?" Her stormy eyes held me.

"Yes," I answered.

Mary put her arm around Leslie's shoulder and led her out the door. Leslie didn't even turn to look back at me. And I was left alone in the kitchen. I listened to the distant sound of car doors slamming, an engine starting, and the slow backward grind of tires going down the driveway. I sat in the chair across from where Mary had been, and I swear to God I didn't move for an entire hour. Until Mary came back, opened the door, and then I began to cry.

"When do you expect your mother?" she asked, oblivious to my tears.

Had I been younger I would have blubbered, "Oh, please don't tell my mother, please, please." That's what I wanted to say, but I only looked at her with that in my eyes and said, "Ten, I guess. Around then."

"Well, I'll tell you what. I'm going to go upstairs and pack, and while I do that—"

"Pack?" I stopped sobbing and looked at her hopefully. "You're going home?"

"No, I'm not going home. I lost my job, thanks to you, and I've got to get out of here tonight." She glanced at the clock. "Ted gets off duty tonight at three, and I don't know if Leslie will be able to keep this secret. She's too upset." She pressed her weight into her knuckles and leaned across the table, drawing closer and closer to me. "But before I leave, you and I and your mother are going to have to talk. You're not going to get away with this, Robin. I want to be sure you know what you've done."

I didn't want to know. I didn't want to know and I didn't want to care, because I knew it wasn't good, not good at all. I dropped my head on my arms and I didn't hear her leave the room. I listened to my breath echoing off the table near my face.

15

Mary and I didn't speak another word to each other until Ma finally strolled in at ten thirty. Mary's things were already packed in her car and she was fixing herself a cup of tea at the stove. I had taken up my post at the kitchen table like a sick animal. I didn't want to move. I nearly slept with my head down on the oak table, and my sneakers and socks were in a circle around me on the floor, as if it were an ancient ritual—a slaughter.

"Whew!" Ma dropped her bags and boxes and packages right inside the door. She looked happy and glowing, and I thought dully that Tom had probably been with her. Well, she wouldn't be glowing and jolly for long. "So! How's stuff?" It was like Big Bird walking into a morgue. The silence stopped her dead in her tracks, and with her fingers poised on the front of her half-opened coat she stared first at me and then at Mary. "What is it? What's the matter?"

"We need to talk, Janet. The three of us. And then I have to leave. I'm packed. I'll be leaving tonight."

Ma slid her coat off her shoulders and threw it over the back of a chair. "All right," she said softly. "Something's wrong. Why don't we talk about it. Come. Let's sit inside." She looked at both of us. Mary nodded, picked up her mug of tea, and walked out of the kitchen into the living room. I pulled myself out of my death seat and straightened my stiff knees.

"I have to go to the bathroom," I said, and without touching Ma or looking at her, I slipped past her to the little bathroom off the kitchen. I stared at myself in the little wood-framed mirror. I listened to the lonely sound of my own water and I pressed my fists into my eyes. I wished I were dead.

Mary and Ma were waiting in the living room. Mary was in the rocking chair, and I thought how she had probably never been in our living room before, but she sat there as if it was natural, like she did it all the time. She sat back relaxed, with her legs crossed and her hands cupped around the mug of tea in her lap. Ma sat on the couch, on the edge of her seat, still in her good boots, still with a silk scarf wrapped around her throat. I sat next to her, facing Mary.

"I have something to tell you," Mary began. She rested her head back and closed her eyes. I thought, like her daughter, she would open them again slowly, but she kept them closed. "I have a husband and two children in a house in Willowtown, 24 Dubbin Lane. My children are Leslie, twelve, and Timmy, seven." I felt Ma glance at me. "My husband is a police sergeant with the city police force. And we've had a problem."

She began rocking and she stopped talking. I stole a glance at Ma, and I could tell she was totally lost. This wasn't at all the way I would have told the story. Mary sighed, coughed, and then opened her eyes. She still didn't look at us.

"My husband is a good man, or he *was*. We'd had a lot of good times, until his drinking got bad." She stared off into space, lost to us. "He always liked an occasional beer, and even when I first met him, he enjoyed hanging around with his friends at the neighborhood bar, but then, I don't know. It all changed. All of a sudden he couldn't handle things anymore. He was drunk a lot. And his job was getting to him—his superiors, his beat, the union." She shrugged. "Everything was going wrong. And then one night he came home all worked up. He was't himself." She rubbed her fingers over her eyes roughly. Her skin seemed delicate, as if it would crumble. "I don't understand what happened, I don't understand. But he wasn't making sense and I tried to talk to him. I tried to reason with him. . . ." A sad smile curled her lips. "That was the first time. He hit me three times in the head with his fist. I think it was three. That's all I counted. And then I passed out."

I couldn't look at her. I lowered my eyes and I could see Ma's hands clasped in her lap like a vise. Her breathing was controlled and steady.

"When I came to, he was over me crying his heart out, carrying on as if it were the end of the world. He was so sorry. He didn't go to work the next day. We walked around the house with our arms around each other, scared and sorry. I didn't go to work all that week because of the bruises and the bump on my forehead. I didn't mind, though. I always liked staying in. I felt safe.

"But things didn't get any better. They got worse. And the drinking got worse. I felt as if I had my nose inside a bottle of whiskey all the time. If he wasn't home I could smell it on the sheets, in the laundry basket. It was always with me." A tear ran down the side of her nose and over her lip. She didn't move. "I thought I was starting to go crazy. I felt afraid all the time. And I was so scared for Timmy and Leslie." She made a little steeple out of her fingers, pressed them to her lips, and took deep breaths. I waited. "Not that Ted would ever hurt them. No, it was only me he took it out on, but I was scared for them being with me. Sometimes I couldn't remember things. I'd approach a traffic light in the car, and I couldn't remember if red was for stop or go. Some days after they were in school, I'd go back to bed and try to sleep after being up with Ted all night the night before. I'd wake up at three when they got home. They were always angry at me. Timmy once asked me why I was so bad that Daddy had to hit me all the time. I knew the kids saw and heard what was going on. I tried to hide it, but Ted would get so loud. Cursing . . . yelling . . ."

"But Mary, you don't have to tell us this."

Mary looked at me then with shiny eyes. All of her rage seemed to be drained away. Her voice was weak. "Yes, I *do* have to tell you. You both have to hear this, but especially Robin."

Ma looked at me. I felt as if my body were shrinking with shame.

She leaned forward and clasped her hands between her knees. She went on. "This one day I had to go to the hospital. I had pains in my ear. I told the doctor I had fallen in the bathtub. It turned out my eardrum was broken. Ted bought me a new winter coat for that one. Anyway, while I was at the hospital, I guess someone didn't believe my story, because they sent in a counselor to see me. I liked her. And I started to go to see her, even after I left the hospital, every week. I didn't tell Ted, of course. He would have been furious. He didn't want me to tell anyone. He'd say he'd handle it himself, said we'd work it out somehow without having to let anyone know. But it was getting worse all the time. Worse and worse.'' She leaned back now and rested her head. "With this counselor's help, I came up with a plan. I decided to leave him. And the children.'' Mary sobbed, and her hands flew to her face.

I could barely breathe. I didn't want to cry. I had no right to, but tears ran down my face as I sat there motionless. This was the part I hadn't understood, the part about leaving Leslie and Timmy.

When she began to speak again, her voice sounded stronger. "I knew I didn't have a job or a place to live, so that was the first thing. I applied for nursing jobs at a few hospitals, and then once I heard for sure about the job at Mercy I found a room to rent, this room here, with you.''

Mary sat forward and stared down at her hands that were spread open like stiff starfish in her lap. She had changed her bloody dress, and she was in jeans and a sweater. "My plan was to work hard and do well at the hospital, to make sure it would be a permanent position. I was going to save money and get a decent apartment locally somewhere, and then my counselor had given me the name of some lawyers, and I knew once I had a home for my kids, I would see a lawyer and try to get custody of them.''

"That sounds so good, Mary,'' Ma said, and I wanted to put my hand over her mouth. "There are all kinds of groups you could get help from, the Women's Coalition, the Battered Wives—''

"It was all going fine,'' Mary interrupted, "until Robin went in my room and read my journal, went through my personal things, and decided to take things into her own hands.''

"What?'' Ma stared at me as if she had just heard that I—what? What could be worse than what I had done? Mary made it sound so awful. "Robin, *what* did you do?"

It wasn't *all* wrong, what I did. I knew it. I had good intentions. "I went to see Mary's daughter."

Ma collapsed back into the sofa. "Oh, Robin," she whispered. I thought she was going to cry. I already was.

Mary spoke very low and rose from the rocking chair. "I called home this afternoon to tell Robin that I couldn't get home as planned, because there'd been an accident, a nursery school bus with a dozen little children, and I was needed at the hospital." She crossed her arms over her chest. "But Robin told me I had to get home. There was an emergency here. My daughter was here at the house."

"Oh, Robin." I couldn't look at Ma at all.

"So I left. I just walked out. My supervisor said if I walked out, I was fired, but all I could think of was Leslie here, knowing where I was, the whole plan wrecked, everything I had worked and tried so hard to build, destroyed. I walked out on my job and ran home here to Leslie."

Ma was still as death beside me. She hadn't moved, and I half expected her to reach out and slam me. I was trembling. I thought I was going to throw up.

Mary slipped her coat on slowly. She looked at the both of us while she buttoned it up. "I have to leave now. Leslie will probably tell Ted where I am, and I can't see him again till I have some kind of legal protection. And some kind of sanity in my own head so I can deal with him." She pulled her pocketbook over her shoulder. Her face was lifeless. Lifeless, that was the only word I could think of, as if every last bit of life had been wrenched from her as she spoke. "I have to start over again

now. Another job, another place to stay." She
walked slowly out of the living room and paused
in the darkened dining room. I couldn't see her face
clearly, just her silhouette from the kitchen light.
"If Ted calls, you can tell him I left suddenly and
that you don't know where I've gone. You'll never
see me or hear from me again." And she turned
around and left.

"Oh, Robin," Ma whispered in a stricken voice
after we heard the back door shut. "How could
you do such a thing? What were you *thinking*?"

"I thought there was a chance for them to be
together," I said. "I didn't realize she had a plan
to get the children. I thought she had just left them.
I thought she would never see them again. That
was wrong. Parents shouldn't leave their kids.
Never! They should never leave their children. When
you have kids it's your responsibility to be there if
they need you, to never go away, to never, ever
leave—" Tears were running down my cheeks, my
nose was running, and I didn't even care.

Ma was looking at me closely. "Sometimes parents have to—" she started, but I screamed, a loud
monster movie scream to drown out her words.
And I ran up to my room.

My death seat changed from the kitchen chair to
my rumpled unmade bed. I felt a deadening come
over me and I just sat there. I thought of *Moby-
Dick*. I was Queequeg on the deck of the *Pequod*
when he decided to die, and I was sitting with my
arms and legs in relaxed surrender, and the distant
look of a cold dead frog in my eye. I was Queequeg,
and I was willing myself to die.

Later Ma came up, but I was already almost dead.
I don't remember what she said. I couldn't hear
her through the whaling vessel death fog, but I felt

her cover me with my quilt and I heard her turn out the light. It didn't matter. My mind was empty. There was no more Leslie or Mary, no more me, or Ma or Dad. No more bikes, or catalogues, no more nothing, just the beckoning swell of the night ocean.

16

*L*ike *Queequeg*, I wasn't dead the next morning. I was disappointed. Unlike Queequeg, there was no dramatic crisis to raise me out of my stupor, just the dull pesty sound of Ma sticking her head in and out of my room. It started early and I heard her yelling things about school, about being late, about my responsibilities. I wouldn't move. I felt that if I woke and didn't move a single muscle of my body, my brain would think I was dead and just shut down. I thought idly of what it would be like to try to get to school. How would I be able to go to school if I couldn't put one foot in front of the other? I'd get stuck on the corner and not be able to go forward or back. I pictured a big tattooed Queequeg standing there on the corner of Morris and Lakeview with a harpoon in his hand, staring straight ahead.

I can't even say I had any feelings at that point about what had happened the night before. Just a dull numbness, and that was good enough for me. That's what I wanted. Nowadays I can think about Leslie and wonder how it all eventually worked out, but not that morning. Thinking about what I had done would have been like squeezing a glass Christmas tree ball really hard between the palms of my hands. All I wanted to do was to avoid the crunch and the pain of it.

Ma's appearances at my bedroom door went from

displays of teeth-gritting anger to mumbling worry. Soon she was standing over my bed pressing her palm against my forehead. I pushed her hand away and lay there staring at my desk.

Eventually I got out of bed for no other reason than I couldn't bear her concern another minute. I went down the stairs like a sleepwalker and walked into the kitchen numbly, not even caring how cold the linoleum was under my bare feet. I could hear her talking to my father on the phone. I heard her say his name, and I heard the concern in her voice, and the confusion. It interested me as much as the salt and pepper shakers on the table. I sat down and rested my head on my arms in my comfortable old seat from last night. Mary, her stiff words, her painful accusations, and her sad story flitted through my mind like a cloud of gnats, and I smashed them all. I made my mind a blank again. Ma was standing in front of me, and the phone was back in its cradle.

"As long as you're not going to make it to school today, Daddy wants you to come spend the day with him," she said. "We'll make today your annual day off, okay?"

It didn't make any difference if I answered or not. I knew they had decided I'd go there, and it didn't matter to me. Ma stood there waiting for an answer that wasn't necessary.

"Robin!" she shouted. "Stop this! Say something!" In two strides she was around my side of the table and her fingers were digging into my shoulders, and I could smell the coffee on her breath. "Don't do this, you hear me? What's the matter with you?"

"Nothing. Nothing." I shrugged her off, pushing her away. I remembered seeing a dying seagull once down at the beach, and a dog had played with

it, torn at it, and the seagull just flapped around
feebly, not seeming to care, as if she were thinking
of something else and couldn't be bothered knowing that her leg was being torn off. Ma's hands
pulled back from me, and then she reached out
again and tucked a hair behind my ear. I brushed
her hand away.

"Robin," she started, pulling up a chair close to
mine, "why don't we talk about what happened?
I know you didn't mean anything bad by what you
did. I know your intentions were—"

"Any bagels?" I asked.

Her mouth tightened into a nasty line, and she
glared at me. "Robin, I can't have this! Now I
understand you meant no harm, but we can't let
this go by without some kind of discussion, maybe
a punishment—" She shook her head. "I don't know,
but I do know we are not going to pretend this
didn't happen. Interfering in Mary Walker's life
was unacceptable behavior."

"Have we got any pineapple jelly?" I asked.

Ma stood up stiffly. "Get your own jelly." She
was breathing hard, threatening to cry. "I refuse
to speak about this any more today, but when you
come back from your father's we will sit down and
hash it out. Is that clear?"

I opened the refrigerator and fished around for
the jelly. It wasn't till she left the kitchen that I
found it where it always was, right on the shelf on
the door.

Instead of dropping me off at the front door, Ma
parked the car and walked me to Dad's apartment.
We rode the elevator silently, just as we had driven
in the car. When we got off the elevator, I heard
Dad's door open, and he was standing there wait-

ing. A vague thought crossed my mind that Ma had never been in Dad's apartment.

We stepped inside and he shut the door quietly. The three of us just stood there. I remembered being little when Ma was into making my dresses and I had to stand very still for what seemed ages while she pinned my hems. That's how I felt. Like they were pinning my hem and I couldn't move.

Ma and Dad reached across me and I heard them kiss each other's cheeks. I didn't look. I kept watching out his window at a flag waving on a rooftop about two blocks away. I let my hands hang at my sides. I was too tired to put them in my pockets.

"I haven't been able to talk to her about it," Ma said as if I weren't there. "I tried, but she won't open up." Ma walked past us into the center of the room. "I don't know what to do. It's very serious, what she did. We can't just let it go by and not deal with it. And yet I can tell she feels awful—"

Dad was slipping my coat off my shoulders, and for a few seconds he disappeared down the hall. "Leave her here, Janet. Maybe she and I can talk. We'll see." He didn't take her coat, but stood there looking at her in the middle of his living room, where she had never been before. I thought of being younger and standing my Barbie doll on the radiator to see how she looked, and then on my bed, and then on the edge of the tub, on the ladder of the pool. I stood her everywhere in every outfit to see how she looked in different places. That's how Dad was looking at Ma standing there in the middle of his living room. I looked back at the flag. He slipped his arm around my shoulder and led me to his couch.

"Sit down, Bird. I was just going to make some tea. Could I get you a cup?"

I shrugged. He didn't ask Ma, and I noticed she was easing herself closer to the door. "I'd better go," she said. "I told them I'd be late at work, but I don't want to get there after lunch."

I couldn't see the flag from the seat on his sofa, but I could see an airliner far, far up, streaking across the sky as slow as a star. I watched it move, lining it up with the panes in the window, and by the time it was out of sight, Ma was gone and Dad was in the kitchen, making noises with spoons and cabinet doors.

"How many sugars?" he called.

"Three," I answered.

I heard him grumble, and then he appeared in the living room with a nice heavy mug in each hand, each one steaming and hot. He sat beside me and handed me the mug. I wrapped my fingers around its warmth and watched the steam rise. I could hear him sip his noisily while it was still hot.

I had always liked the sounds in his apartment, the different heat noises in the floorboard radiators, the distant clang of the elevator doors opening and closing, and on a windy day, the sound of the wind brushing past his long windows. We didn't speak at all, and when my tea had cooled a little, I sipped it. I could tell he hadn't put three spoonfuls of sugar in it, but it tasted okay and I finished it.

All the while his one arm was around the back of the sofa, just barely touching my shoulder. I hadn't even looked at him since I arrived, not close, not his face, but I closed my eyes and imagined him. That's hard to do, to try to exactly picture someone's face in your mind without a photograph or something. There are other things I can conjure up more easily, like the sight of his hands on the steering wheel of our old car, and yet I knew he didn't drive much anymore. I could see him tapping his ring on the wheel while he waited for a light. I could see clearly his two shoes next to the side of his bed, I could see the careful way he always brushed crumbs from the table with the side of his hand.

When I put my empty cup on the table next to a framed photo of him and me, his hand came down on my shoulder. We didn't say a word, but I drew closer to him, and then it was so easy to lay my head down in his lap, with the back of my head up against him. He patted my head like I was an old dog, and like an old dog, I felt forgiven.

17

"*Do you want* to talk about it?" he asked.

"I don't know. I don't know where to start," I said. I stretched my legs out on the sofa, and pushed my sneakers off my feet. They fell to the floor.

"Why did you go into that woman's room to start with? How about that? Help me to understand what was behind that."

"Did you ever see her?" I asked, actually picturing Mary in my mind for the first time without flinching.

"No, but both you and your mother had said how nice she was."

"Yeah, she was nice, but she was sad mostly, you know, like there was some kind of terrible sadness in her life. You could see it in her eyes, and these kind of sad lines in her face."

"You have some imagination, Bird."

I sat up and looked at him. "But it wasn't my imagination! There *was* a terrible sadness in her life. And I knew it when I saw those pictures of her kids, and when I read her journal." I lay back down in his lap and heard him sigh.

"How about you?" he asked.

"What—how about me?"

"Do you have a 'terrible sadness' in your life?" His hand kept patting my head.

I thought about that. Things were all right at

school, I wasn't retarded or anything, and life in my house was okay, Ma was all right most of the time. His hand felt so comforting and loving stroking my head. I could feel love in his hand. I could always remember feeling love in his hands, and then I realized what my terrible sadness was. And I started to cry. I cried hard, like I had seen little kids cry when they scrape their knees. I turned over and buried my face in his chest and held onto him with all my strength. I was afraid I was going to fall off the face of the earth, as if everything that was holding me down had just snapped and I was going to go hurling into space, lost and broken.

He held me tight against him, as if he knew I would fly away, and I felt his arms holding me back on the sofa in his living room. I knew I could let it all out as long as he was holding me there. I cried for a long time and he never said a word. After a while I was exhausted and wet. His shirt was wet from my tears, and my hair was stringy and sweaty. I collapsed against him and felt empty, like I was totally drained of air and blood.

"What is it, Bird, huh? What is it?" he whispered.

I didn't have to hide anything anymore. All along I had been pretending I was so brave and mature and understanding and everything, when I really didn't understand it at all. "Do you love me, Daddy?" I whispered.

"Yes."

"Then how could you leave me? How could you just leave me like that, Daddy?" I thought I was all cried out, but my eyes filled with tears again.

"That's what we thought," he murmured to himself. And then he looked at me. "You've been *too* good through this separation and divorce, you know that?"

I didn't know what he meant. He shifted his weight, and I sat up and leaned against him. I started to talk. "You know, I've seen movies where parents get separated from their kids, where they get separated by a river in their rafts, or else they're slaves and a mean slave owner sells them off, away from each other, or even Anne Frank, knowing she got taken away from her parents like she did, and every time I see something like that I cry, it's so sad. And then you left." I looked in his eyes, to accuse him, or question him, I wasn't sure.

"You just left. No raging river. No mean slave owner. No Nazis. You just decided to leave. I can't believe it. And we never kissed each other through chain-link fences. I never ran after a train you were on. You just left."

"I didn't 'just leave,' Bird. It wasn't that simple."

"It seemed that way to me. Everybody kind and polite and you packed up your things and gave me a calendar with when I could see you, and your phone number with where I could reach you. I mean, you're my *father,* for God's sake, Daddy, and you just walked away, like it was so easy."

His face was solemn.

"And you didn't even cry! At least Ma cried sometimes, but with you, nothing. I kept wondering if you left because you couldn't stand my orange peels in the TV room anymore, or if you hated class plays, or rock music, and you were just so relieved to be rid of me."

"Robin," he said, so sad. "Moving out of the house was one of the hardest things I ever had to do."

"It was? Then *why* did you do it?"

"Because the other hardest thing was to go on living with someone who didn't love me anymore, someone I had stopped loving, too."

"Ma?"

He nodded.

"But you could have tried, Dad. You could have tried harder to love each other. I read in the magazines how there's all kinds of things you can do to save a bad marriage. And you and Ma didn't have a bad marriage—"

"Robin." He put the tips of his fingers on my mouth to silence me. "You don't know. You really don't know, and I know you think you can read minds, and change the world and make everybody do what they should do, but you don't know everything. Can you accept that?"

I didn't answer him. No, I couldn't accept that.

"Hasn't this bad experience with the boarder taught you something?"

I thought of Mary and how she was running away again now because of me.

"Sometimes from the outside we think we can see what someone should do with their life, but we're not in that person's head. There's no way we can really ever know what someone has to do. Now that woman had lived a life, and she had to come up with her own solutions that could only work for her. There was no way that anybody, including you, could interfere in that and take it over."

"But—"

"We all have to walk our own walks, Robin. Your interference didn't work, did it?"

I shook my head.

"And from what I hear, what you did has made

things worse, not better. You know that, don't you?"

I nodded. "I feel terrible about the girl, about her daughter."

"Yes," he said. "I'm sure that's going to be something that will be hard for you to live with. But you know what, honey?" He squeezed my arm. "You didn't create that situation in that family. They had their problems long before you ever heard of them, and they're going to have problems for a long time to come, whether you had gotten involved or not. And you know what else?"

He took my face between his hands and squeezed my mouth into a funny shape. He smiled. "You had nothing to do with what happened between Ma and me. Nothing. How many times do I have to tell you that?" He pulled my head close into his chest in a headlock.

"Yuk! You're all wet," I told him.

"Wonder why, wonder why." He laughed. And then he drew away to look at me. "And did you really think I didn't cry?"

I shrugged. "I don't know. I never saw you cry."

"I cried," he said. We looked at each other tenderly. He would probably never cry in front of me, but I believe he had cried. But now he laughed again. "Slave drivers, huh? Nazi camps, and chain-link fences, and disappearing locomotives fading in the distance. My, my, Bird, what a mind."

"Don't laugh at me," I said. "I don't think it's funny."

He was instantly serious. "I'm not laughing at you. I'm sorry. It's just we try so hard to do everything right, and there's no way, absolutely no way to help anyone through a crisis except to stand by and let them walk through it. I'm sorry my leaving seemed too easy, too casual, and not dramatic enough for you. It was painful for me, as painful as if I'd been tied up and carried away on the back of a slave wagon. I want you to believe that, but I also want you to know I had a comfort, Robin, a real comfort."

He sighed and we held each other. "I knew I was losing a part of you, that daily, everyday part that you get from living with somebody, but I knew I'd never lose you entirely, like slaves or prisoners, or lost rafts. I guess that's why I made a big deal about the calendar and how easy it would be for you to reach me. I guess I tried to minimize what I'd be losing."

It was all so sad, and we sat there for a while, simply holding each other close and soaking in all that had been said. Suddenly he rubbed my arms swiftly like he was trying to warm me or get me started again. "Hey, tell you what."

"What?"

"How about we rearrange all my furniture today? I'm getting bored with it this way. I think I need a change, and you look like a nice strong gal." He felt my muscles. "What do you say?"

I looked around his apartment. It looked nice. It looked like him. "Oh, I don't know."

"What! What do you mean, you don't know? I thought you were dying to rearrange this joint and make it more efficient."

"Yeah," I said, "but I don't live here. I don't know what's the best way to arrange stuff. You know. It's your life. You decide. Right?" I asked, as if I were checking on something new I had just learned.

He smiled at me. "You're right, but the difference here is I'm asking you to help me, got it?"

I nodded sheepishly.

"And believe me, if you come up with any cock-amamie ideas that I don't think I could live with, I'll tell you. Is it a deal?"

"A deal."

We shook on it, and he was true to his word. He liked my idea about putting the bookcases around the sides of the windows, but no way was he going to let me put his mattress and box spring on the floor. And he even asked me to go to Macy's with him and help him pick out towels and a shower curtain.

I got to sleep over that night, even though it was a week night. We decided we needed a little "daily time" together, and although I didn't talk to her myself, Ma agreed.

18

I guess it would be really nice to be able to tell you at this point that I had learned a lesson, made some changes in my thinking, and gone on to lead a happy, normal life, but there's more you have to know. Oh, sure, things were a little better with my father. Not that they were ever bad or anything, but we were closer, more "daily" about each other.

Ma and I got along okay. Once in a while I'd see her watching me, as if I were a stranger who had just wandered into the house. She'd always been so concerned about doing the right thing, and always talked about feelings, and communicating. But we didn't talk about Mary anymore, or Dad either, for that matter. It can be comforting to talk about sadness, or anger, and try to work things out, but sometimes what you're really feeling is total confusion, and the only way confusion can be worked out is simply to let it swirl around in a glass until it settles, and once it's settled, then you can look at it and count the layers and the sediment and try to figure it out. Ma doesn't always understand that, but at least she had backed off a little, and I felt like I had some elbow room. I guess on some level she had given up on me—not that she didn't love me anymore, but she suddenly realized I wasn't five anymore, and I was having my own feelings about stuff, and finding my own answers.

I left her alone about Tom, too, so I guess it was some kind of loving standoff, if there is such a thing.

Anyway, what was left of this ordeal happened just a couple of days before Christmas. Ma and I had put up the Christmas tree together. When I was little I remembered that every year we would add something new to the tree. Once we baked salt dough cookies and painted them. And then one year I made clothespin people. This year Ma was busier than ever, and I knew it was up to me. I decided to string popcorn and cranberries. They would only last this one year; they wouldn't last forever, but then what would? It seemed a meaningful decoration for that particular Christmas.

Ma and Tom were going to go out for dinner at some fancy restaurant somewhere, and even though I had been invited, Alastair Sim was going to be on that night in *A Christmas Carol,* and I didn't want to miss it. It was Dad's favorite movie, and I had promised him I would watch it. Both my parents are nutty like that, forcing me to watch their favorite movies, as if they were an important part of my education.

The phone rang at seven while Ma was getting dressed, and I answered it. "Scroooooge! Scroooooge!" said a spooky voice.

"Hi, Dad. I didn't forget."

"Just thought I'd remind you, Bird. Don't want you to miss it."

"I've got my popcorn all ready and some hot chocolate," I told him.

"Well, don't get fat now," he cautioned.

"I'm not going to eat the popcorn, I'm going to string popcorn and cranberries for the tree."

"Oh."

"Dad?"

"Yes?"

"Remember that little Christmas tree ornament you gave me when I was four?"

"The bird?"

"Yeah, the one you picked up in Africa?"

"Sure, what about it?" he asked.

"I don't know. I was just wondering if you remembered it, that's all."

The doorbell rang.

"Listen, I gotta go. That's Tom at the door," I said.

"What?" he scowled. "Are there no prisons? Are there no workhouses?"

My father can be so funny sometimes, especially since he's usually not very funny, so when he does make a joke it's good, like he's been saving up for a big one. Through my laughing, we said goodbye and I ran to let Tom in.

I opened the door a crack, and peeked out. "What?" I said when I saw Tom standing there. "Are there no prisons? Are there no workhouses?"

"Alastair Sim!" he cried. "*A Christmas Carol,* nineteen fifty-one."

I opened the door wide and let him in. I hadn't meant to be so friendly. "Wrong." I scowled. "Charles Dickens, eighteen forty-three."

He slipped his leather gloves off and stood there smiling at me. "Ah, but you sounded just like Alastair Sim. Sim says, 'Are there no prisons? Are there no workhouses?' Whereas Dickens wrote it, 'Are there no prisons?' And then he adds, 'And the Union workhouses? Are they still in operation?' See? You have to know the difference."

"Gimme a break," I said, closing the door. I

noticed the snow starting to come down outside, like a Christmas movie.

"Besides," he said, "isn't Charlie Dickens a country-western singer?" He tapped me on the head with his gloves as I passed. The duel was on.

"You're thinking of Charlie Pride," I said, "but you're way off. *Pride* was a novel by Jane Austen . . . *Pride and Prejudice*."

"No, no, no, you're wrong. It wasn't Austen, it was Jane Fonda. And I'm awfully fond o' Alastair Sim."

"Ah!" I shouted. "You did it too fast. Too fast." I ticked them off on my fingers. "Alastair Sim, Charles Dickens, Charlie Pride, *Pride and Prejudice*, Jane Austen, Jane Fonda, Alastair Sim. That's only seven. I once did forty-three with my friend, starting with Tom Selleck, then it went tomcat, Sears catalogue, Sears Roebuck, Buck Henry, Henry the Eighth, eight ball, Lucille Ball—"

"Hi, Tom." Ma came into the TV room, interrupting me just in time, before I started having too much fun. She looked really terrific, and I saw the look on her face when she smiled at Tom. Tomcat, I thought. But I looked at him, and he had a pretty nice-looking smile, too. Inside I shrugged. There was nothing I could do. If she wasn't going to hold out for Sylvester Stallone, there was nothing in this world I could do about it. That wasn't exactly something I could talk to my father about, but I knew he would be proud that I had figured that one out on my own.

"Be careful driving out there in the snow," I said, as Tom helped Ma on with her coat.

"Listen to that, would you?" Ma laughed. "My teenage daughter fussing at me about driving." She shook her head. "Your turn will come, my dear," she said. "Just you wait. Can I stay out past midnight, or is the curfew on tonight?"

"How long is it going to take you to eat?" I asked. "Not four hours, that's for sure." I turned on the station for *A Christmas Carol*.

"Are you sure you don't want to come with us, Robin?" she asked. "It's not too late, you know."

"Nah. I promised Dad I'd watch *A Christmas Carol* tonight, and besides I have miles and miles of popcorn and cranberries to string before Sunday."

"*A Christmas Carol* is on tonight?" Tom's whole face lit up.

"Uh-huh."

"With Alastair Sim?"

"Yep."

"Oh, Janet," he said, suddenly looking worried. "I really think the roads are pretty bad tonight. Maybe we should just stay here and send out for a pizza."

Ma ignored his comments and turned him to face the door. "Good night, Robin. Enjoy your movie and we'll see you later."

Tom shrugged and winked at me. What a jerk. I tried not to let him see me smiling as I bolted the door behind them, and watched through the glass doors as they disappeared into the night like two figurines in a glass ball filled with a warm, swirling snowstorm.

The house was so quiet and peaceful, and a little bit spooky, too. It's a big old house, and you can be in one room and not be able to hear someone speak in another room. You can't even hear the doorbell sometimes from upstairs, and from my room, you definitely can't hear my mother calling

from the kitchen. I walked around while I waited
for seven thirty and the movie to begin. I stopped
at each window and looked out at the snow. The
wind was starting to whip around like crazy, and
I thought of all the little kids who were excited
about the snow, all the kids who knew that tomorrow night Santa would make it in his sleigh
because there was snow on the rooftops. I remember believing stuff like that, and then choosing not
to believe it on the years it didn't snow.

I gathered up my bowl of popcorn, the bowl of
cranberries, and the mug of hot chocolate and
brought them into the TV room, setting them down
by the light. Then I brought in the sewing basket
with the threads and needles. I felt so domestic and
cozy. I slipped off my sneakers and threw an afghan
over my lap. The theme song for the movie started,
and I sighed with pleasure. I guess it was the kind
of moment I would be nostalgic about all my life.
And I knew even at that moment how good it was.
I didn't realize though how I would never, ever
forget that night as long as I went on living.

I had barely gotten used to the black and white
of the old movie when I heard a loud thump and
a crash outside. I jumped up and ran to the window,
and I remember actually thinking—"And out on
the lawn there arose such a clatter, I sprang from
my seat to see what was the matter." A big heavy
branch had fallen from the large maple in the front
yard and had crashed to the lawn. It was not completely down, though. It had gotten snagged on
some wires. I turned back and looked at the lights.
It wasn't the electricity, although I could see sparks
jumping through the flurries of snow. The phone.

I ran to the phone and lifted the receiver to my
ear. Dead. I almost cried. I knew my father was

going to call when the movie was over, and he wouldn't even be able to get through now. I worried that he would get a busy signal and think that I hadn't watched it at all. "I'm watching it, Dad," I mumbled to myself. I hung up the phone, went back to the TV room, and picked up my string of popcorn and cranberries once again. The knocker on Scrooge's door was the face of Marley. Not too scary. I had seen too many *really* scary movies to be scared of a knocker. Dad said I was jaded. Fourteen years old and afraid of nothing.

I was just getting into the movie when I thought I heard muffled footsteps slowly coming up the front porch steps. I waited and listened. Maybe I was wrong. I hadn't heard Tom's car, and they weren't due back for a while yet. It occurred to me to peek out the window, but with all the popcorn mess in my lap, I decided against it. I kind of didn't think about it, as if maybe my mind was playing tricks on me, what with the scary movie and stormy night and all.

I went on stringing and then I knew I definitely heard a noise on the front stoop. I dropped everything on the floor next to me and just listened. Why would someone come up on the front stoop and not ring the doorbell? A shiver ran up my spine, and I froze. The sounds didn't seem like normal footsteps. They were too slow, a slow heavy clumping, like something being dragged, or lifted and then dropped.

I always used to have bad dreams about what I'd do in a situation like this, and always in my dreams I would be paralyzed, unable to move, or if I did move it would be so slow as to be entirely useless. Now, wide awake, I was relieved to discover I could creep along with the sureness and control of a cat. Step by step, with my stocking feet sinking silently into the thick rug, I crept to the door. The porch light was on outside, and there was no light on in the hall where I stood. I knew I would be able to see out, and no one would be able to see in.

Without disturbing a pleat or a hem of the curtain on the inner glass door, I touched it gently and put my face right by the molding. Ever so quietly, I began to pull the curtain back so I could see. I moved like the workings of a clock, slow and nearly motionless. To my horror, what I saw was the back of a large man, leaning on the glass windows of the outer door. My instinct was to say, "Hey, don't lean on that door. You'll break it." Ma didn't even allow my friends to use the front door, it was so precarious with its heavy beveled glass windows. Now there was this stranger leaning on them and about to fall through into the vestibule. I was scared. I don't think I've ever had a dream where I was as scared as I was at that moment. Even nowadays when I dream about that night, nothing matches the fear that I felt then. And when I remembered that the phone was dead, it was as if someone had thrown ice water in my face. I knew I wasn't going to be like those jerks in the movies who open the door and say, "Hey, what's the matter?" Not me. There was no way I was going to open the door or do any of the stupid things I had seen done so many times. I checked up and down the outer door. The bolt was on and the chain was on, and I knew it was locked from the outside as well. Even with the bolts on, though, it was only as safe as that glass was strong.

I was horrified to see the man pull his weight off the door. The glass seemed to shift in its molding.

He disappeared from my view for a second, and I realized by the sounds and the sudden movement that he had staggered off away from the door. He returned, facing the door, and fell into the side of the house. He was obviously very drunk. I had always laughed at drunks on TV, funny men reeling about, taking funny steps, leaning into things, moving slowly and carefully, doing things almost too deliberately, as though they had to aim their bodies ahead of them. It didn't seem funny anymore.

I couldn't see the man's face. I had no idea who he was. There was no rumor at school about strangers or perverts around lately, so this guy wasn't someone who'd been making any touble that I knew about. He wore a heavy green army type coat with a big hood pulled down over his face. The hood was lined with fur, and I could just make out the tip of his nose. He wore gloves, and a scarf, and I could tell by the sound of his steps that he was wearing heavy boots, the noise I had heard dragging across the front porch floor.

The man lifted himself from the wall of the house and found the doorbell. He pushed his fist into it, jamming, jamming the bell. The punching noises scared me, but he wasn't good at doorbells and it didn't ring. I was frozen to the spot, my finger looped in the curtain, my face pressed up near the window. I didn't want to stay so close, and yet I couldn't leave, as if my very presence would keep the glass from breaking in.

He began to talk to himself. I couldn't make out the words at first, but then he began to call in a loud voice, and I felt the horror of it all come crashing around my head like an avalanche. "Mary

Ellen!" he growled. "Mary Ellen! Come out! I know
you're in there!"

It was Mary Walker's husband, Ted. The policeman. It was Leslie's father, drunk and heavy at
my front door. Now, you have to believe I wasn't
going to let him in, I swear it. I had no intention
of that at all, but so much of this was my fault,
right? Here he was, looking for her because of me.
Leslie was probably very upset because of me, and
now Ted was here, and I was getting all these crazy
feelings like the whole situation was my fault.

I told Dad later that I really didn't have any of
those old feelings like I could fix everything and
make it better. I knew that was impossible. I even
understood a little better why Mary had left, seeing
her husband this way. It wasn't funny, ha-ha, Dean-
Martin time. It wasn't tipsy, or half lit, or anything
cute. It was drunk—heavy and violent and destruc-
tive, and I could almost smell it through the door.
But I wanted to tell him that Mary wasn't here
anymore. I wanted to clean the slate and send him
away honestly, once and for all.

I double-checked the bolts and the chain on the
outer door as he continued to punch the doorbell.
Once or twice the bell made a weak noise in the
kitchen. Pulling myself up as tall as I could, I took
a deep breath, calmed my hands, and unlocked the
inner door. That was as far as I was going to go.
I stepped into the vestibule with the double glass
door between us. He squinted at me and pulled his
hood off his head to see me better.

"Mary Ellen here?" he said.

"Mary Ellen doesn't live here anymore, Mr.
Walker. She moved out and she didn't tell us where
she was going." I tried to sound reasonable and

sane, but I felt like I was telling a hungry dog that I simply wouldn't be able to feed him until the groceries were delivered.

Ted Walker narrowed his eyes and placed his fist on the heavy window. "I want to see Mary Ellen," he said. "Get her down here, right now."

"She's not here anymore, Mr. Walker. She's really not. She took all of her things and—"

"Get her!" he screamed, and he kicked the bottom of the door.

My legs were turning to jelly, and trying to look as if I wasn't moving at all, I started backing up, never taking my eyes off him.

"Get that bitch down here, and tell her if she's not down here in two seconds, I'm going to beat the ever-loving shit out of her, you hear me?"

I nodded. Crazy, the things you do. I kept backing up, little steps, feeling the door with my hand, stepping back into the doorway, turning slightly to close it before me, and then with trembling hands I bolted the inside door, tight and secure. I don't know how long I stood there with my hands over my mouth, chattering, "Oh no, oh no," over and over again. It was like I knew just what was going to happen. And I did. At exactly the right instant, I touched the curtain again with my fingers and drew it aside. I pressed my face to the slit in time to see Ted Walker punch through the heavy glass window and break in the door with a kick.

19

I flew back away from the doors to the wall at the end of the front hall. I don't know what I was waiting for, but I had this delicate refined sense of waiting, like a condemned prisoner must feel while he waits for the rifles to click. I didn't breathe, didn't move, and I don't even think my heart beat for those few minutes. I can't tell you how weird it is to feel safe in your own home, to feel cozy and protected, like you're in some kind of fort or something—even the TV was still flickering away as if nothing was happening—and then all of a sudden your front door comes crashing in.

There was one loud kicking smash against the inner door, then another, and the door opened up, still locked tight, but taking a hunk of molding off the wall. Ted entered like a marionette, walking a peculiar flat-footed gait. Gently he turned and closed the door behind him, smoothing the splintered wooden molding into place with his gloved hands. I stared at his back, thinking in one instant of all sorts of things, like hitting him over the head with a chair, a bottle, giving him the Vulcan death grip, but I couldn't move. I was terrified he would come after me, and all I wanted was for him not to move, just to stay right where he was.

He turned and rubbed his eyes as if the dim light in the hall was too bright for him. I realized how cold it was and how long he must have been outside. There was ice on his mustache, and his eyes were tearing. "I'm terribly sorry," he started, "but I have to see my wife." He spoke politely, as if he hadn't just broken in the front door.

"She's not here, Mr. Walker," I said again. I was pressed against the wall. If I ran to the left I could get to the kitchen, and maybe out the back door. If I ran to the right, I could run up the steps and lock myself in my room or in the bathroom. He lurched toward me and leaned on the wall, blocking my way to the kitchen.

"Don't give me that," he slurred. "She's been pulling this on me for too long. Don't give me that shit. She's my wife, and I have every right to see her." He reached out his hand as if to touch me, but he misjudged how far he was and his hand fell back against his leg. I took a step away from him.

"I'm not lying to you," I said. "She left Monday when Leslie found out where she was. She was very upset and she left."

He slid along the wall closer to me. "I know you," he said slowly. He was squinting at me, studying me. "You're the kid with the Christmas cards and stuff."

I tried to be light and airy. "Yeah! That's me. Mrs. Walker bought some cards from me, and you paid me the day I delivered—"

"Did you know where Mary Ellen was that day? When you saw me?" He had pulled a flat whiskey bottle out of his deep pocket and tilted it up to his mouth. "Did you? Huh? Huh?" His voice echoed in the bottle.

"Yeah, I knew, but I didn't want to say anything—"

He slammed his fist into the wall and the painting

above him jumped on its hook. "Why didn't you tell me then, you stinkin' kid!"

I moved closer to the stairs and he matched me move for move. "I wanted to, but I wasn't sure. I wanted to help. Hey, listen, I was on your side. I really was. I wanted to get you all together, to get her back again so you could work out your problems—"

"What problems?" he roared. "We didn't have any problems. What did that bitch tell you?" He was coming after me, and I took a leap toward the stairs. I had to get away from him. I had to lock myself away from him. But as I leaped and started to scream up the steps three at a time, his hand wrapped around my ankle and he pulled me back down. My knees and elbows crashed on each step and I reached out to grab the banister, to hold on to something. He twisted my leg till I was facing him.

"Where is she?" he asked through clenched teeth. He put his face close to mine, and I thought I'd die from the smell of the whiskey. I squinted up my eyes and pulled my hand over my face. I couldn't speak.

"Okay, little lady," he said, "let's go look for her." He dragged me to my feet, and grabbing a handful of my sweater in his fist, he pushed me up the steps, bellowing all the while, "Mary Ellen! Mary Ellen!"

I would show him Mary's room, show him that it was empty, and then I would break away and lock myself in the bathroom. He pushed me from behind, jamming his fist into me, and he stopped before each bedroom. "This isn't it," I'd say, and he'd push me to the next doorway. I stopped in front of what had been Mary's door. I suddenly remembered standing there nearly two months ago, making my decision to go in and to pry into her things. Oh, if I could have gone back and redone things. "This is where she stayed when she was here," I told him. "But she's gone."

I opened the door and he pushed me into the room. I reached out and turned on the light. It was too bright. I felt exposed and in danger. I looked at him cautiously. He took me along with him over to the closet and opened it. It was empty. He walked to the bed and lifted the uncovered pillow to his face and smelled it. He threw it back. "She wasn't here," he said, his face clouding over. I tried to be smaller, tried to disappear into my clothes, shrinking, fading.

"She was," I told him again.

"Where is she?" he growled. He dropped his hand from his grip on my sweater, and before he could even get it halfway to his pocket to pull out his bottle, I was flying from the room and into the bathroom that I knew would lock securely from the inside.

I heard his footsteps. I heard him coming. The door slammed shut behind me, and in an instant reflex motion, I turned the key under the doorknob. I could hear my heart pounding in my ears. I could hear him coming out into the hall, and then I heard what sounded like his body rubbing on the outside of the door. "Get out here," he slurred, "before I come in and get you, you hear me?" It sounded like he had begun pounding lightly, threateningly on the door with his heavy fist.

I stood on the tub, unlatched the window, and opened it wide. Then I opened the aluminum storm window. The snow was coming down heavily. I cupped my hands around my mouth and yelled, "Help! Help!" as loud as I could but the snow muffled my voice, and I felt as effective as Olive Oyl. I could tell my call didn't even travel as far as the edge of the eaves, under the window. But he heard me. The pounding grew louder, and I panicked. Without thinking twice, I lifted myself to the window ledge and scooted out the window. The pounding grew louder and louder. I could hear wood tearing, things crashing, breaking. It was brutally cold, worse than jumping in a lake in May, but I tried to ignore the cold and I pressed myself up against the scratchy shingles of the house. My socks were wet from the snow, and my toes began to sting from the cold. I was shivering.

Then I heard the bathroom door break open and his heavy footsteps on the tile. I listened. I didn't move. "I don't need you, you dumb kid," he snarled. "I'll find her without you, you little bitch. I don't need you to give me a grand tour in here." I heard glass break on the bathroom floor, and I scrunched my shoulders up and put my hands over my ears. Staring out into the pine tree near the house, I thought how the next time I took a bath, I'd have to be careful of any bits of broken glass Ma might miss when she swept up. And then I just grew numb. There was a nagging thought that I might never take another bath again. Suddenly the bathroom window slammed shut, and I heard him turn the lock at the top.

I was locked out of my house, on a ledge outside the bathroom window. It was snowing, and I was petrified. There was no way to get down, no drainpipes, no trellises. And no one would hear me no matter how I yelled that night. All my polite neighbors were sealed inside their houses with their double-layer windows, and even if someone was out walking a dog, my voice was trapped in those thick snowflakes as if I had a bandanna over my face.

I moved cautiously to the window and peered into the brightness. I watched him pick up large pieces of his broken whiskey bottle and throw them in the sink. He stumbled from the room and disappeared down the hall. I kept my arms across my chest, trying to keep warm. One foot stood on the other trying to keep dry. I couldn't believe where I was. I looked around. I was familiar with that old roof. I had been out there many times on summer nights, one night in particular, I remembered, when I climbed out my window and sat on my sleeping bag to watch an eclipse of the moon. The roof was at a steep slant, but not so steep that I couldn't maneuver easily along the outside wall of the house.

Slowly, carefully, I edged my way along to my own bedroom window. Sometimes I feed birds out my window, and if I had been really careless and sloppy about it last time, I would have left the storm window open and the inner window unlocked. I had. I was suddenly so grateful that I was such a slob. I had to tell Ma. I had to tell her it was okay sometimes to be a slob, and that everything would work out for the best.

As quietly as I could, I slid the wooden window up in its tracks. I couldn't tell where Ted Walker had gone. Was he still on the second floor looking for Mary? Was he even in my room looking for her? I stuck my head in the window and listened. The warmth inside made my eyes water. I couldn't hear a thing. Slowly, I opened the window all the way, and put my leg in the room. A pile of my books toppled over, and I froze. But nothing happened. He didn't come charging into the room. I stepped over the books and pulled my other leg in after me. I could see the broken bathroom door lying in pieces right outside my door.

My socks were sopping wet, and I silently pulled each of them off and stood there, listening for sounds. I thought I heard him downstairs. Yes, I heard the sound of cabinet doors opening and closing in the kitchen. I crept out into the hall and leaned over the banister.

"Where the hell do they keep the booze in this house?" he was mumbling to himself. More doors opened and shut. I heard a kitchen chair toppling over and some things fall off the countertop onto the floor. He cursed. Dad always said Ma piled things too high on the countertop. Pots and dishes and glasses were always precariously balanced. Now they were all over the floor. I could hear him kicking things in anger. I had to get out of there and get help.

I edged my way along the second floor railing to the stairs. I was going to have to go down there and get past him. Eighteen steps and all of them had their own little creaks. I was barefoot now and I stuck close to the wall, one step at a time. I leaned my weight against the wall with one hand, and on the banister with the other. I was very quiet. I mentally pictured myself walking down the steps without even touching the carpeting. I could levitate and fly to a neighbor's house.

Halfway down I heard his footsteps leaving the kitchen and coming into the dining room. Once in the dining room he would be able to see the stairs, see me. Forgetting about being quiet, I flew down the rest of the steps and ducked into the living room. I wasn't sure if he had heard me or not. I heard his fist on the china cabinet and Ma's good stuff jingled inside like a Christmas bell. I dove under her rolltop desk and wrapped my arms around my legs. I was a statue, a stone. I could have stayed in that position forever. I pressed my face into my knees and tried to breathe quietly.

"Mary Ellen!" he shouted at the top of his lungs. I tensed so hard I could feel cramps starting on the tops of my legs, but I didn't move. "Mary Ellen! Mary Ellen!" It became like some kind of awful song. Then he was quiet. He was in the living room. There were no lights on and I could see him silhouetted against the dining room light. He was very still, and I grew even more frightened. I thought he sensed I was in the room. I thought he smelled me or saw my foot under the desk. But then he began to whimper. "Mare, Mare, Mare," he cried. "Come on, baby. Come on out, sweetie babe. I won't hurt you. Come on, babe." He walked in a slow circle around the living room. I could see he was slapping his hands against his eyes and then against his legs. His eyes, his legs, his eyes, his legs. Like a madman. My leg started to tremble and knock against the desk. I held it tighter.

"Oh, babe," he cried. "Where'd ya go? What's the matter? Come on, Mary Ellen, we can talk, like you want to. We'll talk. I'll get help. I promise. I know this is crazy." He started to cry hard. "I know this is crazy. I don't know what's the matter with me."

I watched his heavy footsteps come close to me. He moved toward the sofa, where he kicked aside the small table and fell on top of the needlepoint pillows, over the crocheted afghan, and on top of my Othello game. "Oh, Mare, oh, Mare," he moaned.

I didn't breathe or move. If I had reached out with my hand, I could have touched him. I could have touched his arm, the sleeve of his heavy coat. I stared at him in horror, waiting.

Soon his crying stopped. The sobs and wails subsided into deep horrible sighs and then—I couldn't believe it—he began to snore. Every nerve in my body was ready to run, to go screaming from my familiar living room in horror. I unwound my arms and crept slowly from beneath the desk. He continued to snore. I crawled across the floor toward the kitchen, afraid to stand up and draw attention to myself. I crawled until I was in the kitchen, and then I stood and acted as if I was going to take out the garbage. I was cool. I opened the door to the laundry room very quietly and shut it behind me. I took the key down from the nail by the back door and put it in the keyhole at the first try. I wasn't even trembling anymore. I was beyond that. I unlocked the door, unbolted it, opened and shut it, and then I began to run across the backyard. And it's funny, but all I can remember thinking was, "Hey, I'm running barefoot in the snow. I never did that before. That's a new one."

20

I ran toward a light in the swirling snow, the
house behind ours, not even caring that I didn't
know the people who lived there. We had one of
those nodding relationships, you know, where
you're mowing the lawn and they're mowing the
lawn and you nod and smile at each other over the
racket of the gasoline motors. I think once my
father had spoken to someone in that house about
the poison ivy growing along our mutual fence,
but that must have been over three years ago. I
climbed over the fence, my bare feet stinging in
the snow, not even feeling the toe holds I took in
the woven redwood. The fence swayed slightly
under my weight. I never looked back. I didn't
know if Ted Walker had heard me go out the back
door, but picturing him right behind me made me
go faster than I ever thought possible.

I ran up the back steps of the house and pounded
on the door. Suddenly I couldn't wait another minute to be warm. The checkered curtain parted
slightly, and an unfamiliar face peeked out at me,
an older woman. She just looked at me, blankly.

"Let me in!" I screamed. "Let me in! Help me!"
The curtain fell back in place and the door didn't
open. Now I looked over my shoulder back at my
house. No one was chasing me. No one was coming down my back steps, over the fence, across the

yard. Maybe. It was hard to see through the curtains of snow. I pounded on the door. "Help me!"

Then I heard footsteps inside, and the curtain parted once more. This time a man peered out at me. "What is it?" he asked through the glass.

"Please let me in," I cried. "I have to call the police. A man broke into my house. There's a man in my house. Please. Please let me in."

I heard the bolt on the door, and it opened into a warm checkered kitchen. I nearly fell into the room, and they closed the door and stood there staring at me. They were an old couple, probably married for a hundred years, and I could tell they didn't know what to make of me.

"I'm Robin Lewis," I began. Suddenly it was so important that they like and trust me. "I live in the old Davis house behind you there. You know, the house with the poison ivy along the fence. I see you sometimes when I'm mowing the lawn." I pointed meaninglessly through the door. "Can I call the police? There's a man in my house, a drunk man who broke in, and I have to call the police and Ma and—" I started to sob. A weird exhausted sob, where I just stood there and wailed. Before I knew it, the old lady had me wrapped in a blanket and tucked me into a chair before the television set in their living room. On their TV was a funny plastic flower pot decorated with plastic doilies and a red feathered bird. I stared at it while I cried, and then I heard the old man dialing his phone. I heard him asking someone to send a police car right over, because he thought there was some trouble in a neighbor's house, and he had a young barefoot woman hysterical and freezing cold in his house. I remembered thinking I wasn't really a young woman, and was I hysterical? I tucked my bare feet up under me in the folds of the blanket.

We waited together, the three of us, hardly saying a word. The old lady gave me a glass of hot chocolate that I sipped while my hands trembled and shook. I dropped my eyes from the weird plastic bird to the TV screen. It was the end of *A Christmas Carol*. Alastair Sim was with a bunch of laughing happy people. The snow was swirling outside, and everyone was filled with joy and holiday spirit.

I had never seen Ma so white before. Or her eyes so huge. She stayed close to me, always touching me somehow, either an arm slung over my shoulder, or her leg against mine on the sofa, or else she'd just hold my hand. I don't think I'd held her hand since I was six. I didn't mind.

It was nearly midnight by the time the police left. They had gotten Ted Walker out of the house and down to the county jail. I never even knew there *was* a county jail around here. The cops told us that he'd be arrested for breaking and entering and a few other things, and that seeing he was drunk, he'd probably be forced to get into some kind of alcohol recovery program where he might get some kind of help. They had shrugged and sneered and left as if it were all kind of hopeless. I thought of Leslie and her skinny legs and her worried face. I hoped he would get help.

The police had also sent a car down to the Lincoln Inn to bring Ma home. I shudder to imagine that scene, her sitting there with Tom enjoying their holiday dinner and in walk a couple of cops with their badges and guns, and, "You'd better come home. There's been some trouble at your house."

But I was glad the police brought them home. I was glad I had guessed the restaurant right, and as I sat there wide awake on the sofa, I was even glad Tom was there. He was kneeling in the hallway, hammering and banging at the broken door. I watched as he measured some pieces of wood, sawed them by hand, and then fitted them roughly against the heavy beveled glass panels. He was making the house safe for Ma and me, safe so we could sleep securely through the night. It's weird, but even though it was late, the last thing I felt like doing was sleeping.

Suddenly the phone rang and shattered the air like broken glass. Ma sprung from her seat beside me and ran to the kitchen. I listened. "Hello? Oh, Len. No, no, she didn't watch the movie. I know. I know. The phone's been out of order. Something awful's happened . . ."

I slowly unfolded myself and walked across the dining room rug to the kitchen where my mother stood with the phone clutched on her shoulder like a shrunken fiddle. There were dishes and pans all over the floor. Two of the chairs were turned over. I held out my hand to her. Everything felt unreal, as if I were walking through water.

"Wait, Len, wait. She's right here, she wants to talk to you herself. She'll tell you. Everything's fine now. It's okay now."

I held the phone to my ear. "Dad?"

"Bird! What is it? What's the matter?" he asked, and I loved the sound of his voice. I felt safe and protected and loved.

"You know the boarder we had?" I asked.

"Yes, of course. Robin, you didn't do anything—"

"No. I didn't do anything, really. I was just

watching *A Christmas Carol,* and her husband came looking for her." I stopped and walked into the dining room with the long cord to get away from the chaos Ted Walker had created in the kitchen. I could see Tom kneeling at the door, tapping lightly with a hammer on nails, my mother kneeling next to him, her fingers holding some wood in place.

"Well, you know better than to let a stranger in. Robin, you didn't—"

"He was drunk, Daddy, and he broke the door in."

"Jesus Christ," I heard him mutter.

"He was looking for Mary, and he didn't believe she had moved out already even when I told him."

"Were you all alone?" he asked.

"Yeah. I was here by myself."

"Did he hurt you, honey? Are you all right?"

I hadn't even thought about that till now. I knew my ankle hurt from when he dragged me back down the stairs, but I hadn't looked at it. I pulled up the leg of my pants and looked. "He hurt my ankle, but it's not bad. Just a bruise. I can walk on it." I found myself laughing. "I had to run barefoot through the snow to the people behind us. Their name is Baker. They're real nice, Dad."

"Is that all?" he asked.

"Is that all what?"

"You're not hurt any worse than a bruised ankle and frostbitten toes? Are you sure you're all right?"

"That's the extent of the injuries," I said, thinking of the cops and their way of talking.

"Do you want me to come there tonight, Bird? I can be there in an hour. I'm sure your mother wouldn't mind. She might even be grateful to have me there just for tonight after all this upset."

I looked in at Ma and Tom. Now she was picking

up big hunks of glass and putting them in a bag.
She looked small and pale and frightened. Tom put
his tools aside and helped her, holding the bag for
her, his head nearly touching hers, and then he laid
his hand on her shoulder and said something quietly
to her. I couldn't hear what it was, but by the low
murmuring sound, I knew it was gentle and caring,
and I saw her smile very slightly and look at him.

"No, that's all right, Dad," I said. "We'll be fine.
We're just cleaning up the mess the guy left, and
then I don't know. I'll probably just go to sleep or
something. I don't know. But we'll be just fine.
Really. Maybe tomorrow you could come out. How
about that?"

"Are you sure?" he asked. "I don't mind."

"No, that's okay. Really. I'm fine now. I'll see
you tomorrow."

"Let me talk to your mother then, okay?"

"Sure. Good night, Dad. Sorry I didn't get to
see all of the movie. I saw parts. Even saw the end
at the Bakers'. They were watching it, too."

He sighed and said, "Good night."

"Ma," I called. "Dad wants to talk to you."

I handed the phone to her and walked to the hall
to admire Tom's patch job. "What a mess," I told
him.

He looked at me and smiled. "It'll be good for
keeping out bogeymen and gorillas for tonight,
anyway," he said. "I think you're going to need a
new door, actually three new doors." He unlocked
and locked the inner doors, swinging them on their
hinges and testing the locks. I wandered into the
TV room, watching my feet, careful of leftover
glass pieces we might have missed.

It was late but I wasn't tired. Getting into bed
was the last thing I felt like doing. I knew I would

lie there wide awake like a doll with her eyes painted open. I flipped through the TV guide. One o'clock. Channel five. *March of the Wooden Soldiers.*

I snapped on the set and turned to channel five. Then I sat on the sofa, where the night had started for me, and picked up my bowls of popcorn and cranberries once more. Tom wandered into the room and stood with his hands in his pockets, staring at the TV.

"March of the Wooden Soldiers," he said.

"Yeah. I hate this movie," I said. "I've seen it about forty-three times." I threaded a needle with a long run of thread.

"Me too," he said. He sat down beside me on the sofa, and I handed him the needle and thread. "Thanks," he said. And then he reached into the bowl and began sewing the popcorn and cranberries with me. It was a dumb movie, the kind you can't stop watching because you can't believe how dumb it is.

Soon I heard Ma hang up the phone and come to the hall. She stood before the doors, running her hands up the splintered boards. She sighed. "These were such beautiful doors," she said. "What a shame."

"Shhh!" Tom scolded.

She came into the TV room with her arms folded across her chest. I threaded another long length of thread and knotted the end securely. She stared at us and then at the TV. *"March of the Wooden Soldiers?* I hate that movie."

"So do I," Tom and I said together.

Ma sat down on the floor by our feet and leaned back on the sofa between us. I handed her the needle and thread. She scooped a handful of popcorn out of the bowl, put it on the rug beside her, and stared gloomily at the TV.

Tom smiled at me, and then dropped a light piece of popcorn on one of Mom's curls. She went on watching the show, her head moving ever so slightly as she strung piece after piece of popcorn. Tom gently placed puffed kernel after puffed kernel on her head, and they all just stayed there like snow-flakes. "What a stupid movie," Ma mumbled to herself.

I wasn't going to give him the satisfaction of laughing. Besides I was too tired. "You're a jerk," I told him. "A real jerk."

And we smiled.

ABOUT THE AUTHOR

Pam Conrad was born in New York City and attended the High School of Performing Arts, Hofstra University, and the New School for Social Research. Novelist, poet, and free-lance writer, she lives with her two daughters in Rockville Centre, New York. Her first novel for young adults, PRAIRIE SONGS, was recently published by Harper & Row.

Electric * Tender * Fresh
Exciting * Romantic * Alive

STARFIRE

☐ **THE FRIENDS**
by Rosa Guy   26519 $2.50
To 14-year-old Phyllisia, the city, her new home, is hard
and cold and filled with cruelty. City life's no picnic for
Edith Jackson either, struggling to survive on her own.
What Phyllisia and Edith need is a friend. What Phyllisia
and Edith need is each other.

☐ **VERY FAR AWAY FROM EVERYWHERE ELSE**
by Ursula Le Guin   25396 $2.50
Owen and Natalie are different from other people. They're
outsiders—brilliant, talented, full of dreams . . . and lonely.
Until very far away from everywhere else, Owen and
Natalie find each other. VERY FAR AWAY FROM EVERY-
WHERE ELSE—a love story you'll never forget.

☐ **SUMMER OF MY GERMAN SOLDIER**
by Bette Greene   25901 $2.75
To Patricia Ann Bergen, 12 years old and shy, the summer
seems a hot, dry, endless wasteland of loneliness. Until
the day she meets Frederick Anton Reiker. Patty and
Anton—a young Jewish girl and an escaped German
prisoner of war—their friendship was very special . . . and
very dangerous.

☐ **LUDELL**
by Brenda Wilkinson   26433 $2.50
Meet Ludell—she's in the fifth grade. And even tho' times
are hard for black families she's got a lot to be thankful
for: a real, true friend, the best grandmother ever, a secret
boyfriend, and her own special joy in living that helps her
overcome the hardships of getting by. Meet Ludell—you're
going to like her.

☐ **LUDELL AND WILLIE**
by Brenda Wilkinson   24995 $2.25
Ludell and Willie—they're going to get married after high
school. Just one more year. But a year's a long time,
especially when Ludell's Mama's so strict. No dances. No
dates. Seems like they hardly get to see each other. Then
Mama gets sick. Ludell and Willie—together they can
handle anything—right?

☐ **WORDS BY HEART**
by Ouida Sebestyen   24272 $2.25
This is a story about love, about faith and violence, about anguish and hope. It is the story of Lena and her father and mother, the only black family in town. It is a story of winning and losing, a story of pride and joy and sorrow . . . and forgiveness.

Prices and availability subject to change without notice.